Miguel gazed down at Leanna with his dark, almond-shaped eyes. "You're very pretty," he said. "Do you have a boyfriend?"

Leanna's heart beat faster. *Don't forget to tell Miguel about Scott—your boyfriend back home in Fair Oaks!* she scolded herself. *You have no business getting excited by this handsome stranger's deep voice and sexy dark eyes.*

But boyfriend Scott was hundreds of miles away.

Leanna looked sideways at Miguel from under her long lashes. *Why not have some fun on my last day here in San Diego?* And as simple as a toss of her long dark hair, Scott and her life back in Fair Oaks were nothing more than a distant memory.

Don't miss any of the books in *Love Stories*
—the romantic series from Bantam Books!

Love Stories

The Language of Love

KATE EMBURG

BANTAM BOOKS
NEW YORK · TORONTO · LONDON · SYDNEY · AUCKLAND

RL 6, age 12 and up

THE LANGUAGE OF LOVE
A Bantam Book / April 1996

Produced by Daniel Weiss Associates, Inc.
33 West 17th Street
New York, NY 10011

ISBN: 0-553-56667-9

Published simultaneously in the United States and Canada

Bantam Books are published by Bantam Books, a division of Bantam
Doubleday Dell Publishing Group, Inc. Its trademark, consisting of the
words "Bantam Books" and the portrayal of a rooster, is Registered in
U.S. Patent and Trademark Office and in other countries. Marca
Registrada. Bantam Books, 1540 Broadway, New York, New York 10036.

PRINTED IN THE UNITED STATES OF AMERICA

OPM   0 9 8 7 6 5 4 3 2

To Carlos, Dora, and especially Leann.

Chapter One

"LEANNA! LEANNA, WAKE up!"

Leanna Van Haver squeezed her eyes shut and covered her head with her pillow. But it didn't help. The shrill screams of her half brothers—no, half *monsters,* she corrected herself— pierced the pillow and stabbed into her eardrums. Tomas and Juan were annoying enough one at a time; it was completely unbearable when they tortured her in stereo.

"I want to go home," Leanna wailed into her pillow. But the muffled sound didn't deter the boys at all as one set of tiny hands began pulling on her arm, while the other tickled her ribs.

"Leanna, wake up! Leanna, wake up!" Their constant chanting was almost as bad as the pulling and tickling.

If my fairy godmother were to appear right now,

1

Leanna thought, *I know exactly what I'd wish for. I'd be home in Fair Oaks, in my own bed, sleeping till noon with the door locked. And Juan and Tomas would be transformed into toads!*

Fortunately, her wish would come true tomorrow. All except the toad part, of course. She was going home to Fair Oaks, California—a suburb of Sacramento—where she could sleep in peace without being annoyed by Tomas and Juan.

Throwing off the pillow, Leanna sat up in bed. "Listen, you little creeps—"

But she couldn't finish the sentence. Leanna's heart melted at the sight of the two small boys, their upturned faces turned toward her adoringly. Tomas, age six, had high cheekbones, dark, tanned skin, and slender limbs. He and Leanna resembled their father, Carlos Malig. Four-year-old Juan was a small, plump replica of his mother, Dora Malig, who was Leanna's stepmother. Both boys were so cute—Tomas looking like a little man, and Juan a brown-skinned angel—that Leanna didn't have the heart to threaten to sell them to the circus, or to give them any of the other hideous punishments she thought they deserved when they were acting particularly obnoxious.

They're just excited. They've never had a big sister before, Dora had explained to Leanna earlier in the summer. And Leanna had understood. Until that summer, she'd known her father, Carlos, only through letters, phone calls, and her mother's stories. Carlos's new wife and sons had always been random faces in photographs.

The Maligs had always lived in the Philippines, while Leanna, her mother, and stepfather had lived in northern California. But now Carlos was teaching in a school in San Diego.

When Carlos had invited Leanna to spend the summer with him and his new family in San Diego, she was eager to meet them all. Eager and nervous, too. Having little brothers was a totally new experience. Back home in Fair Oaks, Leanna's only sibling was her stepsister, Kelli, who was a few months older than she.

Leanna reached out and tousled Juan's hair. "So you guys want me to get up, huh?"

"Yeah," Tomas replied. Juan nodded. "Ma says we can go to the Philippine Festival when everybody's ready."

Leanna grinned. "She did? But I don't want to get up so early. I guess you'll just have to make me."

Shrieking with delight, the boys dove onto the sofa bed Leanna had slept on all summer, rattling the metal frame and rumpling the covers. Leanna tossed a blanket over Juan's head, then pinned Tomas with one hand and began tickling him mercilessly with the other.

"Boys! *Para!* Stop! Leave your sister alone!"

Leanna's stepmother, Dora, appeared in the arch between the kitchen and the living room, her youngest son, two-year-old Toby, balanced on her hip. Dora's dark eyebrows were drawn together in what Leanna assumed was a scowl. Far from striking fear into Leanna's heart, Dora's expression made

Leanna giggle. Her stepmother was much too young and pretty to look fierce, especially with Toby grabbing at her dangling silver earrings.

"I told them to see if you were awake," Dora apologized. "I'm sorry they turned it into a wrestling match."

"I don't mind. Besides, I was winning." Leanna hugged one half brother in each arm. "They weren't bothering me, honest."

"They know better." With a few sharp words in Tagalog, Dora sent her sons scurrying down the hall to their bedroom. Then she smiled at her stepdaughter and said, *"Magandáng umága."*

"Uh . . . good morning?" Leanna guessed. Since she'd arrived in San Diego two months ago, Carlos and Dora had tried to teach her Tagalog, one of the most common languages of the Philippines. Leanna was half Philippine half American, and after two months of mispronouncing every word in Tagalog, she'd concluded that her tongue was part of her American half.

Dora clapped her hands. "Correct! You wait, Leanna, soon you'll be speaking Tagalog like a native."

"But I'm going home tomorrow," Leanna reminded her.

"There's always next year. You can practice with the tapes your father bought you. That way, when he sees you next time, he'll be so proud of how much you've learned."

Leanna didn't reply. It would be rude to tell

4

Dora that she thought learning a foreign language like Tagalog was too much work and not worth the trouble. It would be ungrateful, even cruel, to add that she didn't know whether she wanted to come back next summer. Carlos and his family had done their best to give Leanna a fantastic vacation, but she didn't think of the Maligs as anything more than distant relatives.

Although Leanna had received birthday cards and pictures from Carlos for as long as she could remember, she didn't feel close to him. She'd been a baby when her parents had divorced and Carlos had returned to Manila. And her mother had remarried by the time Leanna had turned two.

Jason Van Haver, Leanna's stepfather, was the only "Dad" she'd ever really known. That was why she called Carlos by his first name—not "Dad" or "Father." Anything else made her feel disloyal to her mother and stepfather. As for spending every summer and some holidays with the Maligs . . . well, she was afraid she might hurt the Van Havers' feelings. And what about all the fun she'd be missing with her friends back home in Fair Oaks?

When Dora turned and walked toward the kitchen, Leanna wondered if she should have said something positive about being there or learning Tagalog. Leanna didn't want to upset Dora. It was just hard to get excited about a language and a culture she didn't understand or know anything about.

Carlos and Dora acted as if they were still in the Philippines. They ate strange foods, most of their

5

friends were Filipinos, and when they rented videos, it was from a tiny shop that stocked Philippine films in Tagalog. Sure, it was interesting to learn about another culture, but Leanna didn't want to make it permanent. One mother and one father was enough. She didn't need another set of parents, another set of rules.

Leanna climbed out of the sofa bed, pulled up the covers, and folded the mattress back inside the sofa. Only one more night of sleeping in the living room, thank goodness!

Padding into the kitchen on bare feet, Leanna saw Dora frying up a pan of *tocino*, or Philippine bacon. Toby, clinging to Dora's leg, was chewing on a strip of dried pineapple.

"Oh, Leanna!" Dora turned, a spatula in her hand. "I didn't hear you come in."

"Mmmm, that *tocino* smells delicious," Leanna lied. Leanna couldn't stand the sweet smell—or taste—of the Philippine bacon. "Can I give you a hand?" she asked.

"Thanks." Dora nodded at Toby, whose sticky hands were wrapped around her leg. "I think he's dirty. The diaper bag is—"

"I know where it is." Leanna pried Toby loose. He let out a wail of protest, but she carried him toward the boys' bedroom, anyway. "When I offered to help, I was thinking of setting the table," she muttered to herself. It seemed as if she'd spent her entire vacation changing diapers. Rather than getting to know her birth father, Leanna had gotten

6

acquainted with the smelly end of a toddler.

"After breakfast, we're going to Balboa Park for the Philippine Festival," Dora called down the hall to her. "We wanted to give you a treat on your last day here."

Leanna groaned loudly. Some treat! Hiking around Balboa Park in the blazing hot sun, eating strange food, and listening to people jabber in a language she couldn't understand! Whoopee!

"Is something wrong?" Dora asked. She sounded genuinely concerned.

For a moment, Leanna considered telling her the truth. Dora—at twenty-seven years old—was only eleven years older than Leanna, more like a sister than a stepmother. She wondered if Dora would understand how she felt. "Yes!" she wanted to shout. "Something is terribly wrong! I miss my mom, my stepdad, my stepsister, and all my friends! I know Carlos loves me, and I want to love him. I want to love all of you, but I hardly know you. I just don't know where I fit in!"

Leanna fastened a clean diaper around Toby's waist, picked up the little boy, and headed back to the kitchen. She'd decided to tell Dora how she felt. But by the time Leanna got there, she found Carlos standing by the counter, wearing a long, embroidered shirt and carrying a wide-brimmed straw hat.

"How do you like my *barong Tagalog*, Leanna?" he greeted her. "It's the Philippine national costume."

"Uh, are you talking about the shirt or the hat?" she asked.

Carlos chuckled. Dora joined in, and even little Toby giggled.

Leanna hung her head. They were laughing at her. She felt so stupid! She was tired of not fitting in, despite her long, jet-black hair and tanned brown skin.

I'm American, she thought. *Why can't the Maligs accept who I am and stop pushing all this Philippine culture down my throat?*

Chapter Two

"**S**ORRY," MIGUEL SARMIENTO told his sister, Carrie. "You know I'm only going to date Filipina girls from now on."

Miguel turned back to his dresser mirror, considering the subject closed. He ran a comb through his jet-black hair. He had to finish getting ready for the Philippine Festival. He'd promised to help sell T-shirts, and his shift began in an hour. But his sister, Carolina—or Carrie, as she insisted on calling herself—wouldn't let the subject rest.

"Since when?" Carrie demanded, planting herself firmly in the doorway of the bedroom Miguel shared with their thirteen-year-old brother, Ramon. "What's wrong with Tiffany? She's my best friend!"

"Nothing's wrong with Tiffany. She's totally hot. Tell her I'll go out with her," Ramon called out from his top bunk before Miguel could answer.

He was on his back, thumbing through a motorcycle magazine.

Carrie threw him a withering glance. "Sorry, loser. Tiffany doesn't date little boys." Turning back to Miguel, she said, "Tiffany's pretty, and you haven't gone out with anyone since Julie dumped you—"

"She didn't dump me!" The comb clattered to the dresser as Miguel whirled furiously toward his sister. "It was a mutual agreement."

"Yeah," Ramon interrupted with a nasty laugh. "You agreed after Julie showed up at the Junior Prom with another guy."

Miguel breathed deeply, not trusting himself to speak. It was true that Julie Bromberg had started dating another guy without bothering to break up with Miguel first. It hurt even more when he thought about how he'd defended Julie to his parents, who didn't like the fact that he was dating an American girl. He'd thought Julie had felt the same way about him. But he'd thought wrong.

He should have listened to his parents and dated a nice Filipina. Someone who cared more about loyalty than about chasing guys with big cars and lots of money. But Miguel couldn't tell Carrie and Ramon how he felt. His sister, with her cropped hair and tight Spandex minidress, and his brother, with his single earring and long hair in a ponytail, seemed to have forgotten that they'd lived in the Philippines just two short years ago. They were in America now, and that was all that mattered.

Miguel shook his head. They'd only laugh if he

10

told them he was afraid to date Tiffany. She was pretty but she was a total flirt. She'd chase any guy who looked her way, and after catching him, she'd get bored and dump him. Miguel knew Tiffany was a player, someone who didn't care about anyone but herself. Miguel wasn't like that, and he didn't want a girlfriend who acted that way, either.

Ignoring Ramon and Carrie, Miguel studied his own face in the mirror. Was he ugly? Was his lean, dark face too skinny? Were his long eyelashes too feminine? Maybe he should grow a mustache. There must be something, some fatal flaw that had made Julie reject him.

"What's with you?" Carrie demanded. "You can't spend your life moping over Julie. Tiffany's available and she likes you."

"She thinks you're sexy," Ramon added with that sly smirk he'd picked up since he'd started hanging around his new American friends. "You should take advantage of it."

"Is that how you treat girls?" Miguel asked. "Take advantage of them?"

"Chill out, man," Ramon said rudely. "You don't know how to have fun anymore."

"Ramon's right," Carrie told Miguel. "It wouldn't hurt you to relax and hang out once in a while."

"I told you, I'm not interested. When I fall in love, it'll be with someone serious, honest, considerate, and old-fashioned. Someone who respects tradition—"

11

"Give me a break!" Carrie interrupted with a loud snort. "You've been listening to Ma and Papa again."

"It wouldn't hurt you to do the same."

Carrie just laughed. "In your dreams! I'm outta here."

"What about the Philippine Festival?" Miguel asked. "Aren't you going?"

Carrie shook her head, making her spiky hair stand out like porcupine quills. "I'll be at Tiffany's, giving her the bad news."

"I'm not going, either." Ramon tossed his magazine to the floor and swung down from the top bunk. "I'm hanging out with Chuck and the guys."

Miguel's mouth dropped open, but for a moment he couldn't find his voice. Ramon and Carrie weren't seriously thinking of skipping the Philippine Festival! His parents were already there, setting up the food and equipment at the park. They expected all seven of their children to show up later, and everyone except five-year-old Joy was supposed to volunteer at the concession stands.

"You have to come," Miguel said. "This is important. Not just to Ma and Papa, but to the entire Filipino community."

As his brother and sister hesitated, Miguel continued. "Besides, Ramon, you shouldn't hang out with Chuck. He's a loser."

Ramon's eyes blazed. "Don't tell me what to do. At least I have American friends." Jamming a baseball cap over his long, messy hair, Ramon stormed

12

out of the room, hands thrust deep in the pockets of the saggy trousers he wore in imitation of the other guys in his rowdy crowd.

Miguel turned to Carrie. But she glared at him. "Don't expect help from me, big brother. First you insulted my friend, and now you're insulting Ramon's. Not everybody can be Mr. Perfect like you," she said as she exited the room. A few minutes later Miguel heard the front door slam.

Miguel rubbed his forehead. He suddenly had a splitting headache. How had things gone so horribly wrong?

I wish we'd never left the Philippines.

For a moment, Miguel felt a sharp pang of homesickness. He missed his grandparents and his friends who still lived in the *barrio* where he'd grown up. He hadn't made many friends here. And once he'd found himself a girlfriend—well, that hadn't worked out.

Miguel looked in the mirror one last time, combed his straight black hair, then tucked his comb in his back pocket. He might be a bit short by American standards, but his tanned arms were muscular. Maybe he wasn't the coolest guy in the world, but at least every girl who saw him today would know where his heart belonged. His brand-new T-shirt, proudly displaying the red, white, and blue flag of the Philippines, made sure of that.

Two hours later, Miguel had sold dozens of T-shirts like his own, but he'd had no luck finding a beautiful dark-haired girl to help him forget how lonely he was. He'd seen lots of pretty girls strolling around the outdoor festival, but most of them were hanging on the arms of other young men. The few girls who'd approached him alone seemed to be buying T-shirts to surprise their boyfriends.

It wasn't fair! Miguel was surrounded by hundreds of people but he felt totally alone. He looked away from the happy couple in front of him. . . .

And found himself gazing at the most beautiful girl he had ever seen.

She was about his age. Her long dark hair was hanging loose, like a curtain of pure black silk, flowing past her slender shoulders to rest halfway down her back. Her profile was like a sculpture: straight nose, delicate chin, each feature perfectly chiseled with a steady hand.

She wore a bright yellow *terno,* an old-fashioned dress with a square neckline and sleeves that stood up like butterfly wings. Her knee-length skirt showed off her smooth, tanned legs. Usually, Miguel didn't get too excited over what girls wore, but this was different. No one his age ever wore such a traditional Philippine costume. Most Filipina girls just wore jeans or shorts.

She didn't seem to see him, though. The beautiful stranger walked purposefully along the path, looking straight ahead rather than at the booths that lined the walkway. Miguel had never seen this girl before, but that wasn't unusual. San Diego was a large city, and lots of people had come from out of town to swell the crowds at the festival.

He was so hypnotized by the girl that at first he didn't notice the baby stroller she pushed ahead of her. Could she be married? No, that plump little boy in the stroller had to be her brother.

Someone cleared his throat loudly. "Wake up, kid! How much for the T-shirt?"

Miguel turned to find a middle-aged man standing at the counter, a white shirt slung over his beefy, tanned arm.

When Miguel finished with the customer, he looked for the girl again. But she had disappeared. Quickly, he turned to his mother's friend, who was in charge of the T-shirt booth. "Mrs. Lisondra—"

"Go, go," she broke in, smiling as she shooed him away. "You've already been here for two hours, and none of the other teenagers volunteered for more than one. There aren't many young people like you, Miguel."

"Thanks, Mrs. Lisondra."

As he hurried up the path in the direction where he'd last seen the angelic girl, Miguel thought that, without knowing it, Mrs. Lisondra had put her finger on his problem. There *weren't* many teenagers who felt the way he did about pre-serving the past.

But with any luck, he was just about to find one more.

Chapter Three

"*AKO SI MIGUEL. Ano ang pangalan mo?*"

Leanna heard the words but continued walking, thinking the deep, musical voice was calling out to greet someone near her. People swarmed around her and in front of her, but Leanna felt invisible. She knew no one here except the Maligs.

At least she'd finally gotten a break from them! All except Toby, and with any luck he'd fall asleep fast. She'd been a dutiful daughter all morning, even agreeing to wear the queer dress with the odd stand-up sleeves that Carlos had bought her. After lunch, she'd volunteered to baby-sit Toby while the others attended a performance of Phillipine music and folk dance. Now she had two hours all to herself.

And she intended to spend it as far from the Philippine Festival as possible. Leanna headed for the other side of the park, hoping to find a playground where she could push Toby on the swings and where the people around her spoke English.

As she continued along the path, Leanna paid little attention to the booths lining the walkway. But then a display of brightly colored shirts caught her eye, and she steered the stroller over to investigate.

Kelli would love this, she thought, running her finger over the soft fabric of a turquoise blouse with silver sequins on the sleeves and neckline. Her stepsister Kelli liked dramatic clothing, and the color would be perfect with her blond hair.

Or maybe one of those beaded necklaces in the next booth would be better. It wasn't as if she *had* to leave the festival. It was actually kind of interesting, Leanna admitted to herself.

"Ako si Miguel," repeated the male voice, this time right at her elbow. *"Ano ang pangalan mo?"*

It's a guy—and he's talking to me! Leanna was shocked to realize. *But I don't know any guys here. Certainly none with such a sexy voice!*

Gripping the handles of Toby's stroller, Leanna turned toward the voice and began saying the first phrase she'd learned in Tagalog. It was the only one she pronounced correctly every time, because she'd used it so often: *"Hindî ko maintindihan."* I don't understand.

Then she got a good look at the stranger, and her words caught in her throat. For a moment, Leanna couldn't think of a thing to say in English, Tagalog, Spanish, or any of the other languages being spoken all around her.

18

This guy was totally cute. His wiry frame was rather short, but he was still taller than Leanna's five feet two. Back home in Fair Oaks, her boyfriend, Scott Carteret, was so tall, she had to lean back just to see his face. It made kissing a real challenge. *Maybe that's why we don't kiss much,* Leanna had thought. Gazing directly into a boy's eyes was a strange—but interesting—new experience.

This guy was probably her age. His face was boyish, but his arms were muscular, as if they belonged on a grown man's body. He must lift a lot of weights, Leanna thought, as she noticed how his biceps stretched the sleeves of his T-shirt. Blazoned below the red, white, and blue Philippine flag that decorated the front of his shirt were the words FILIPINO PRIDE in bold black letters.

It wasn't easy to tear her eyes away from his strong chest. But when Leanna finally managed it, she saw straight, jet-black hair framing a round face with smiling lips and deep brown eyes that gazed mischievously at her.

Switching to English, the boy nodded at Toby. "Cute kid. Is he yours?"

"No, this is my brother Toby." *Does this guy really think I look old enough to have a child?!* "How old do you think I am?" Leanna asked the handsome stranger.

He shrugged. His muscles did interesting things to the flag on his T-shirt as he moved. "Uh, fourteen? Fifteen?"

"I'm sixteen!" There went her hope that she was

19

starting to look more mature. "And I don't plan on having kids until after I graduate high school—*and* college."

She'd meant to put the guy in his place, but he only laughed. "You never know," he said, stooping to pat Toby's head. "You could be from one of the Mountain Tribes. Those girls marry early. At fifteen, a pretty Igorot or Ifugao girl would already have children."

Leanna shrugged. Had Carlos ever mentioned the Mountain Tribes? If he had, Leanna hadn't been paying attention. She desperately hoped this cute guy didn't want to discuss Mountain Tribe customs. Somehow, she was certain a hunk wearing a "Filipino Pride" shirt wouldn't be impressed by her complete ignorance of everything Philippine.

Before she could think of a way to steer the conversation into familiar territory—any subject but the Philippines—the handsome stranger straightened up. He rested one hand next to Leanna's on the stroller and gazed down at her with dark, almond-shaped eyes. "You're very pretty," he said. "Do you have a boyfriend?"

Leanna's heart beat faster. *Don't forget about Scott,* Leanna scolded herself. *You have no business getting excited over this guy's deep voice and sexy dark eyes.*

But boyfriend Scott was hundreds of miles away right now. He'd phoned a few times that summer, but instead of making her feel better, Scott's voice had only made her exile more painful. It reminded her that Scott, Kelli, and all their friends were having fun back in Fair Oaks while she was stuck in San Diego without anyone close to her age. And things between her and Scott had felt forced when she'd last seen him. Could they have been growing apart?

Leanna looked sideways at the hunk from under her long lashes. *I might as well have some fun on my last day here.* "Do I have a boyfriend? Well, that depends on what you asked me in Tagalog before. Was it something dirty?"

The boy laughed, and his eyes crinkled at the corners. "I asked your name, and I introduced myself. *Ako si Miguel* means, I'm Miguel. I'm seventeen, my last name is Sarmiento, and I live in San Diego, but I was born in the Philippines. Now it's your turn. Who are you, besides Toby's big sister?"

Leanna looked down, afraid to meet his eyes. If she introduced herself as Leanna Van Haver, Miguel would surely ask why she didn't have a Philippine name. She'd have to explain that her mother was an American—not a Filipina—and she just didn't want to get into her complicated family life at the moment. Besides, why tell all the personal details of her life to a guy she'd met five minutes ago?

"I'm . . . I mean, *ako si* . . . Leanna Malig." The name sounded foreign and awkward to her ears.

She glanced nervously at Miguel. Could he tell she'd given a phony name?

"Leanna Malig," she repeated firmly.

"Your name is Malig, and you don't speak

21

Tagalog? Your parents should be ashamed!"

Leanna let out a slow, deep breath. "I was born and raised in California," she explained. "I guess my parents wanted me to be completely American."

An unmistakable expression of disapproval crossed Miguel's face. "There's nothing wrong with America, but you shouldn't ignore your Philippine heritage." He waved his arms, a sweeping gesture that took in the Philippine flags, the milling crowds, the bright banners. "*This* is what it's all about."

Suddenly, despite the laughing crowds all around her, Leanna felt utterly alone. Back home at Bayside Academy, she sometimes felt the same sense of isolation. There, she was surrounded by kids whose parents had come from Vietnam, Korea, Mexico, France . . . kids of every shape, size, and color . . . but no one exactly like her. No one who was half Filipina, half American.

"I can't help what my parents did." Leanna willed herself to speak slowly and calmly, but inside she was trembling. Kelli was always accusing her of being too sensitive about her background. Kelli assured her that lots of kids were biracial, and others—including Kelli—had parents who were divorced.

As if sensing her thoughts, Miguel reached out and brushed back a strand of her long black hair. "Hey, Leanna, *Sori po.* Sorry. I didn't mean to criticize your family."

"It's okay," Leanna said.

Miguel's hand rested on the stroller again, but

Leanna could still feel the silky brush of his finger-tips across her cheek.

"So you're not into the Philippine language. What about Philippine food?" Miguel asked.

"Some of it's delicious," Leanna answered truthfully. "I like *adobo*." She didn't add that other dishes Dora served, especially the ones involving ox tongues or tails, made her want to gag.

"What about *lumpia*?" Miguel asked. "I'll buy you some—your brother, too. Or are you too American for that?"

"Oh, we love *lumpia*!" Leanna exclaimed. Dora served *lumpia* all the time. They were elongated egg rolls, stuffed with beef or pork. Leanna had eaten several for lunch less than thirty minutes before meeting Miguel, but there was no need to tell him that. She'd eat *lumpia* until she exploded if it meant spending more time with this handsome guy.

"Here, let me help you with that," Miguel said, taking the handles of the stroller.

Toby made a garbled sound of protest, and Leanna prayed it was baby talk and not Tagalog. She'd never come up with a logical explanation for why her two-year-old half brother knew the language better than she did!

Leanna took out one of the slices of dried papaya Dora had given her in case Toby got cranky and handed it to her half brother. Toby, sticking one end in his mouth, began gnawing contentedly. Leanna hoped the papaya would last a long time.

They strolled past several food stands, but

Miguel seemed to be searching for one in particular.

"So . . . tell me about your life in the Philippines," Leanna began, trying to fill the brief silence between them.

Miguel continued walking. "We lived in a farming village on Luzon, the largest Philippine island. My parents were rice farmers, and we all helped with the harvest. We had a *carabao* named Poni, and I even rode him to school sometimes."

"You didn't have a car?" Leanna asked sympathetically.

"Oh, we had a Jeep. And we lived in a house with electricity and plumbing, if that was going to be your next question."

"Whew, that's a relief," Leanna murmured. For a minute, she'd been afraid that Miguel was stuck in some weird time warp.

"Although," Miguel continued thoughtfully, "I think it would be awesome to live in a bamboo hut in the jungle. Imagine bathing in the river, sleeping on the ground, and picking coconuts right off the trees. It would be so cool . . . like camping all the time. Do you like camping, Leanna?"

"Sure." Leanna smiled weakly. The Van Havers had gone camping a few times, but since Dad and Kelli were allergic to just about everything, they'd stayed in a spacious motor home with comfortable beds and an air-filtering system.

"Did you know there are still some pygmies in remote areas of the rain forest?" Miguel went on. His eyes sparkled, and his smile lit up his face. "I'm going to major in anthropology in college, then I'll go back to the Philippines and actually live in a native village. I'll eat their food, join their rituals, do everything they do. It'll be so cool!"

"It sounds, uh, interesting." Leanna could imagine *vacationing* on a tropical island, inside a nice air-conditioned hotel. But living in the jungle . . . no way!

Anthropologists were people you read about in social studies class. Old people. Nobody she knew at school wanted to be one. Leanna herself hadn't decided what she'd do after college, but she knew it would be something glamorous and exciting. It wouldn't involve drinking from rivers or contracting some rare tropical disease.

Maybe she'd keep on modeling. She and Kelli had appeared in catalogs and fashion shows throughout northern California. Although Leanna's small size meant she was stuck modeling preteen clothes.

Should she tell Miguel about her modeling? Kelli's boyfriends always thought it was cool.

Yeah, right. As if a future anthropologist would be impressed by a teen model. He'd think she was a total airhead!

Miguel broke the silence by laughing. "Sorry. Didn't mean to lecture. Not everyone is into ancient culture, as my brother constantly reminds me."

"No problem. I think it's neat," Leanna assured him. As she followed him through the crowd, admiring his broad shoulders, Leanna thought that somehow deep down, Miguel and she were the same. When Miguel talked about missing the Philippines, Leanna had almost blurted out how homesick she'd been for her family in Fair Oaks. But that was insane. Miguel was totally Filipino, inside and out. He'd never accept her American family.

She couldn't fall for Miguel Sarmiento, Leanna resolved. They lived in completely different worlds.

Chapter Four

"**H**ERE IT IS," Miguel announced, stopping in front of a booth with a red and white striped awning. "The best *lumpia* at the festival."

"How do you know it's the best?" Leanna asked, peering at the woman in a white apron behind the counter. The woman was even shorter than Leanna, and her black hair was streaked with gray.

The woman chuckled. "Every boy thinks his mother's cooking is the best."

"But in my case, most of San Diego agrees with me. Mom's the chef at Luzon Gardens Restaurant," Miguel explained. "Ma, this is Leanna Malig and her brother Toby."

"*Kumustá ka?*" Mrs. Sarmiento smiled broadly and held out a hand to Leanna. Leanna shook it gingerly, as if unsure of what she was supposed to do.

"Ma, speak English," Miguel whispered to his mother. "Leanna doesn't understand Tagalog."

His mother shrugged, looking a little disappointed. Then she greeted Leanna in English and looked over at Toby, who was asleep in his stroller, clutching a sticky papaya shred. "What a little angel!"

"Not when he's awake." Leanna smiled. Pointing to the crisp brown rolls in the pan, she asked, "Are those beef or pork *lumpia*, Mrs. Sarmiento?"

"I made both. Have some of each." Miguel's mother scooped a steaming portion of rice onto a paper plate, then topped it with the hot *lumpia*. As she handed the plate to Leanna, she asked, "Have you ever been to the Philippines?"

"No," Leanna admitted, looking uncomfortable again. "But I'd like to visit someday."

Miguel felt sorry for her. It was one thing for him to criticize his brother, who'd deliberately turned his back on his heritage. While Ramon *chose* to copy the worst in American fashion and behavior, Leanna's parents hadn't given her a choice.

"Leanna likes California, Ma. She's lived here all her life." Miguel helped her out.

"You teenagers all want to be American." His mother's round face looked sad, and Miguel wondered if she was thinking of Ramon and Carrie,

28

who hadn't shown up at the festival. "America is a fine country, but you shouldn't forget the customs of the Philippines."

"That's why I'm here," Leanna said. "I want to learn."

"You should go over to the bookstall. My daughters, Sita and Marta, are working there now. Ask them to recommend a good history book or some language tapes."

"That's too much like school, Ma," Miguel interrupted. He remembered the look on Leanna's face when he'd gotten carried away with his anthropological talk. He didn't want her to think he was a total loser who did nothing but study!

"Hey, let's watch the pole dancing," Miguel suggested. "My brother Noriel and his wife are performing."

Leanna looked startled. "Uh, how many children are in your family?"

"Seven," Mrs. Sarmiento replied. "Noriel, Sita, and Marta have their own families now, so the only ones at home are Miguel, Carolina, Ramon, and Joy. I was the oldest of thirteen children and I helped my mother watch the little ones. I'm happy to see that you help your mother, too, Leanna. How many children in your family, besides you and Toby?

"Well, I—I have two more brothers," Leanna said haltingly. "Tomas and Juan. They're both younger than I am."

"No sisters?" Miguel's mother asked.

"Uh, no, none." Leanna took a quick bite of *lumpia*. "Mmmm, this is delicious!"

Miguel couldn't understand why Leanna seemed so nervous. All he'd done was introduce her to his mother, who was asking questions about her family. . . .

Of course. That was it. She probably thought it was too soon to meet his mother. No wonder Leanna was acting shy. She must think he was moving too fast.

"Thanks for the *lumpia*, Ma," Miguel said, before his mother could ask Leanna more questions. "I'm going to show Leanna more of the festival."

"Good-bye to you, too," his mother said, planting a quick kiss on his cheek. She nodded to Leanna. "It was nice meeting you and Toby."

Miguel grabbed the handles of Toby's stroller and wheeled back onto the path. "I'm sorry about Ma and all her questions," he told Leanna. "She can be nosy sometimes."

"No problem." Leanna sighed. "You and your mother didn't do anything wrong. It's me. Actually, it's my family. They're . . . they're not like yours."

Miguel parked the stroller in the aisle near two empty folding chairs. When he and Leanna were settled in their seats, he asked, "What do you mean, your family's not like mine?"

Leanna twisted a strand of her long black hair. "Well, your family is so old-fashioned and traditional. All those brothers and sisters . . . you must be really close."

"I guess." Miguel picked at a loose thread on the knee of his jeans. If Leanna thought his whole family was so traditional, she'd be in for a shock when she saw Ramon's shaved-on-the-sides, long-in-the-back hairdo!

"I'm not very close to my father," Leanna admitted. "My mom's okay, but she doesn't understand how hard it is for me. I'm the only one in the family who's not—"

"Who's not what?" Miguel asked gently.

Leanna had paused, a look of uncertainty on her face.

"Who's not completely Americanized." Leanna tossed back her hair. "Like, they never told me about pole dancing," Leanna went on. "What is it?"

"It's an ancient ceremony performed at village weddings. See those long bamboo poles on the stage?"

"Oh, the limbo poles." Leanna nodded. "I did the limbo at a party once. It was fun."

Miguel smothered a laugh. She really didn't know *anything* about Philippine dances!

"These poles are held much closer to the ground," he explained. "The bride and groom dance over and between them, while the people holding the ends try to catch their ankles and trip them up."

"That's mean!" Leanna exclaimed, her face flushed.

Miguel thought she looked cute.

"What about smearing cake in the bride's face at American weddings?" Miguel asked. "That's not very nice, either."

"The bride and groom are supposed to *feed* the cake to each other," Leanna corrected him. "It's so sweet and romantic. Only a jerk would rub the cake in his wife's face."

"How about throwing the bouquet?" Michael countered. "Tell me *that's* not sadistic. Crazy bridesmaids kicking and punching each other over a bunch of flowers."

"It's not just flowers. Whoever catches the bouquet is the next to get married."

"You believe that superstition?" Miguel asked.

"Well, I caught the bouquet at my cousin's wedding three years ago, and nobody else at that wedding has gotten married since," Leanna said, looking thoughtful. "I'm not superstitious but I do believe in romance."

For a moment, her dark eyes seemed dreamy and far away. A slight breeze ruffled her hair, and wispy curls fell around her delicate face.

Almost without thinking, Miguel reached out his hand and brushed a silky strand of hair behind Leanna's ear. His strong fingers lingered on the curve of her cheek.

"I believe in romance, too," he whispered. He leaned closer to Leanna, and—

"I wet! I wet!" Toby screamed. His heels

kicked loudly against the stroller's footrest.

Miguel groaned. "Great timing, kid. Couldn't you have waited another minute?"

Leanna knelt by the stroller, a dark curtain of hair falling across her face as she bent over the diaper bag. For once, she was glad Toby needed changing. If her half brother hadn't started yelling, she might have *kissed* Miguel! She should be ashamed, thinking about kissing a stranger when she already had a boyfriend. But she wasn't. She felt like she *belonged* with Miguel. Not only had she almost kissed him, she'd nearly told him about her divorced parents, and about how weird and awkward she felt being the only dark-skinned person in a family of blond-haired Americans.

Leanna finished changing Toby just as the staged wedding ceremony had begun. Toby was usually shy with strangers, but when Miguel held out his arms, Toby climbed right into his lap and snuggled down with a smile.

Leanna found herself wondering what it would be like if *she* were in Miguel's arms. Unlike tall Scott, Miguel was the perfect height. If he opened his arms, she could comfortably step right into them. Their lips would be on the same level. She wouldn't have to stand on tiptoe, and Miguel wouldn't have to bend his back into a pretzel just to kiss—the way she and Scott had to. They could simply lean forward until their lips met.

Leanna glanced sideways at Miguel. His head

was bent as he talked softly to Toby. From this angle, Leanna noticed that Miguel's eyelashes were long and thick, like black velvet. *If I had lashes like that, I'd never have to buy mascara again!*

As the wedding unfolded onstage, Leanna drifted into a fantasy of her own future. What if she and Miguel married? They'd have a beautiful wedding like this one, with flute music and fancy embroidered robes. They'd live . . . where would they live? Not in Fair Oaks, California. There were no pygmies to study. Not in the Philippines, either. No way was she living in a bamboo hut.

Onstage, four men, wearing what looked like short striped skirts, held the ends of two pairs of long bamboo poles. They opened and closed the poles rapidly as musicians played flutes, guitars, and ukeleles. The barefoot bride and groom hopped between and around the four sticks, dancing nimbly out of reach as the skirted men clacked them together. The poles were thin, but when the men slammed them together, the clacking noise was louder than the background music.

"Wow, pole dancing looks dangerous," Leanna said. "I bet you can break an ankle if you get caught between those poles."

If there was one thing Leanna couldn't afford to do, it was to get caught . . . in a hopeless romantic fantasy. Better to give up Miguel—and the

34

Maligs—before they threatened her happiness back home in Fair Oaks. Getting attached meant setting herself up for a pain that would hurt much more than a whack on the ankle.

Chapter Five

"JUST ONE MORE hour," Leanna begged, handing Toby to Dora. She quickly glanced over her shoulder. Good, Miguel hadn't followed her. She hoped he was at the refreshment stand buying the cold drink she'd asked for.

Carlos grinned broadly. He looked so happy, Leanna felt a stab of guilt.

"You're enjoying the festival?" he asked.

"Oh, yes!" Leanna exclaimed. "It's fascinating."

Carlos, still wearing the long, embroidered shirt that looked like a dress, put his arm around Leanna's shoulder. She tried not to flinch, but she was still awkward around him. Even though Carlos was her biological father, he was practically a stranger to her. A stranger in a *dress*! Her stepfather would never go out in public like that.

And Dora's outfit. Dora looked beautiful in her

37

bright blue knee-length tunic with a white lace overblouse. She had white orchids in her hair, and lots of silver jewelry. Nobody dressed like that in Fair Oaks.

Dora flashed a teasing grin. "What did you like best, Leanna? The food, the music, or that cute guy I saw you talking to?"

"Uh, everything," Leanna murmured, feeling herself blush.

"C'mon, Leanna, I want to show you the exhibit on the founding of Cebu," Carlos said, his eyes glittering under the wide brim of his straw hat.

"Thanks, but I wanted to explore some more on my own." Leanna looked past Carlos to cast a pleading look at her stepmother.

"Let her go, Carlos." Dora smiled at Leanna, then added a few words to her husband in Tagalog.

"Meet us by the stage in one hour," Carlos said.

"Thanks." Trying to ignore the deeply etched worry lines that had replaced the smile on her father's face, Leanna hurried back to the refreshment stand where she'd left Miguel. Her heart lifted at the sight of him sitting cross-legged on the grass, holding two paper cups.

"We've got one more hour," she told him, reaching for a cup. She peered inside, then looked quickly away from the disgusting tangle of shredded cantaloupe floating on the surface. "Ummm, cantaloupe punch. It looks yummy!" she lied.

"Can't you stay longer?" Miguel asked. He took a long sip of his own punch.

Leanna shook her head. She had to catch an early flight in the morning, and she hadn't even begun to pack.

"What if I promise to drive you home?" Miguel offered.

Stalling for time, Leanna took a small sip of punch. She was tempted to stay but she *did* have to pack. Besides, hanging out with Miguel in the afternoon was harmless. If she stayed after dark, it would be too much like a date.

"Thanks, but my parents won't let me ride home with someone they don't know. They're very strict."

"Maybe if they met me, they'd let you stay for the fireworks. C'mon, you've got to ask them," Miguel coaxed.

Leanna shook her head. Introducing Miguel to the Maligs would be suicide. He'd immediately figure out that Dora was too young to be her mother, and then he'd know that everything she'd told him about herself was a lie.

"I can't. I told you, my father is strict. He won't let me ride home with guys. I'm not even allowed to date." Leanna paused, feeling a stab of guilt. She shouldn't be saying such bad things about easygoing Carlos. If she'd met a nice boy that summer, Carlos would have allowed her to date him. But then, Carlos hadn't given her the chance to meet anybody. Until now, she'd spent every minute with the entire Malig family.

She glanced sideways at Miguel, afraid she'd

gone too far. What would a guy with perfect parents think of a girl who complained about her father? She half expected him to get up and walk away.

But Miguel wasn't leaving. Leaning across the patch of grass that separated them, he slipped a finger under her chin, tilting her face up gently. "I'm sorry about your dad," he said. "But maybe he'll change his no-dating rule after I convince him that I'm a really great guy."

Somewhere nearby, a bamboo flute was playing, but Leanna could barely hear the sweet strains over the pounding of her own heart. Suddenly Miguel's face—Miguel's lips—were very close to hers, and she was drowning in his soft, dark eyes.

Leanna whispered, "Before you convince my father, you'll have to convince me."

Her eyes closed as his strong yet gentle fingers twined in her hair, drawing her forward. When he kissed her, it was the barest brush of his lips on hers.

She opened her eyes. Miguel was sitting beside her on the grass with his legs stretched out in front of him.

As Leanna started to move closer to him, she uncurled her legs and accidentally kicked over her cup of cantaloupe punch.

"Oh! I'm sorry!" Leanna cried. The spill had narrowly missed her new yellow dress and landed directly on Miguel's lower legs. From the knees down, his jeans were splashed with pulpy orange liquid.

"It's okay," Miguel told her, eyeing the mess. "I'll be right back." Leanna watched as he headed for the refreshment stand to get some napkins.

The spell was broken.

An hour later, Leanna and Miguel sat on folding chairs near the stage, munching tamarind candy and listening to music. Suddenly the Maligs appeared on the path in front of them. Leanna instantly jumped from her seat. She had to get away before Miguel had a chance to meet them.

"There's my family!" Leanna waved vaguely in their direction. "Thanks for everything, Miguel." She smiled sadly. "I'd better go."

Miguel caught her hand and held it. *"Hanggang sa muli,"* he murmured, gazing into her eyes.

"What does that mean?" she asked, feeling the warmth of his hand, the closeness of his body. Part of her wanted to pull away and run; the rest of her wanted to stand there forever.

Miguel smiled gently. "If you can say it, I'll tell you."

Now I know how Cinderella felt, Leanna thought, with a glance at her rapidly approaching family. *Needing to run, but wanting very much to stay. . . .*

She tried to repeat the phrase, stumbling over the unfamiliar syllables. Miguel chuckled softly. She tried it again, more slowly.

"Better," said Miguel. "Almost perfect."

"Now tell me what it means," she urged.

41

"In a way, it means good-bye," Miguel explained. "But since I don't want to say good-bye to you, I've used a formal phrase that translates, 'Until we meet again.'"

But she knew they'd never meet again. It was too late to tell Miguel the truth. Even if he didn't mind that she lived hundreds of miles away, Leanna didn't want a long-distance romance. You couldn't hold hands with a letter. You couldn't take a cordless phone to the prom.

And what about Scott? Poor Scott was back home, missing her, waiting for her. So far, she hadn't *really* been disloyal, Leanna told herself. There was nothing wrong with looking at other guys, talking to them, or even dreaming about them. As for the kiss . . . well, she'd stopped that by splashing Miguel with the cantaloupe punch. Everything she'd done had been perfectly innocent. But if she wrote to Miguel or called him, then she would be actively cheating on Scott. And that wouldn't be fair to anyone.

Leanna pulled her hand from Miguel's. "I really have to go," she mumbled.

Miguel stuck his hand in his pocket, pulled out a pencil stub, and scrawled something on a paper napkin. "Here's my phone number, Leanna. May I have yours?"

Oh, great! What excuse could she give now? If she gave him the Maligs' San Diego number, they'd tell him she lived in Fair Oaks. If she gave him her Fair Oaks number—or the Maligs did—he might call, but then she'd have to explain. And what good was hearing his voice if she couldn't see his face?

"My parents won't let me give out our number," Leanna lied. "They hardly let me use the phone."

"I can't believe they're as bad as you say." Miguel sounded irritated now. "Why don't you let me talk to them?"

"No!" Leanna shrieked. "Uh, I mean, this isn't a good time. My father's in a hurry to get home. His favorite TV show is on soon, and he gets really upset if he misses it."

"Can't he wait five minutes?"

"You don't know my father," Leanna said. Her cheeks blushed from the lies she was telling, but there was no other way. "He has a very bad temper. He holds grudges, too. If you make him miss his favorite show, he'll never let me see you again."

It was the most outrageous lie Leanna had ever told. Carlos had never raised his voice in Leanna's presence, much less gotten angry. Still, it seemed to work. Miguel stared at Carlos Malig as if the man had sprouted horns and a tail.

"I don't want to upset him," Miguel said warily.

"Good choice," Leanna agreed. She felt a hysterical giggle bubbling up inside. She ducked her head, letting a curtain of hair hide her face. "When my dad explodes, it's scary." Without another word she turned and fled, her long hair streaming behind her.

"Leanna!" Miguel shouted after her. "Call me, okay?"

She looked back. For a moment, when she saw Miguel standing against a backdrop of palm trees and Philippine flags, she was tempted to fling herself into his strong arms and confess everything.

No, it was better to forget Miguel. Better to see this for what it was: just a romantic story to share with Kelli when she got home.

"I'll call you," she lied. Then she hurried toward the Maligs without looking back at Miguel again.

She only wished her fairy tale could continue . . . and that it could end with a "happily ever after" instead of a good-bye.

Chapter Six

"**P**LEASE FASTEN YOUR seat belts. Our pilot is beginning his descent. We'll land in Sacramento in approximately fifteen minutes."

The flight attendant's voice went on about gate numbers and connecting flights, but Leanna ignored it. She'd already heard the important part. She'd be home soon!

Leanna folded the in-flight magazine and stuck it behind the seat in front of her. After fastening her seat belt, Leanna turned toward the window. She couldn't see anything except wispy clouds and part of the airplane's wings, but she knew what was down there. Her family. Her mother, her stepfather, and Kelli all waiting to meet her plane.

Scott might be at the airport, too. Unless he had to work. Like Leanna and Kelli, Scott went to Bayside Academy, a private high school for kids who were involved in the performing arts. Tall, gangly Scott wanted to be a movie director. He almost always had a camera or a camcorder in his hand. In his spare time, he earned extra money filming fashion shows at school.

Closing her eyes, Leanna thought about Scott. Some of the Bayside kids—the snobby ones—thought he was weird, but Leanna thought Scott was so different, he was actually cool.

Once, they'd gone to a vintage clothing shop to buy costumes for a school play, and Scott had bought more outfits for himself than he had for the show. Sometimes he wore pin-striped trousers from one antique suit with a checkered vest from another. No matter how bizarre the combination, it managed to look good on his long, lean frame. His straight blond hair was usually falling in his pale blue eyes, hidden behind wire-rimmed glasses. Sometimes she'd catch him staring into space, as if his mind were on a faraway scene he hoped to capture on film.

Leanna smiled, thinking of Scott as she'd last seen him. He was snapping her picture as she'd boarded the plane for San Diego in July. But then his figure blurred, like a camera lens slipping out of focus. Leanna squeezed her eyelids tighter, willing the image to sharpen. But when the picture emerged, the boy in her mind's eye wasn't Scott.

It was Miguel. Leanna remembered his dark eyes, his ready smile, the brief, soft touch of his lips that promised so much more.

46

Her eyes snapped open. *I've got to stop thinking about Miguel.*

As the plane landed at the Sacramento airport, Leanna grabbed her duffel bag from the overhead compartment. One of the first passengers out of the aircraft, Leanna quickly searched the crowd for her family.

They weren't hard to spot. Tall Kelli was jumping up and down. Her neon pink shirt and matching shorts were so bright, she would have stood out whether she waved her arms or not.

Leanna couldn't help smiling. If one word could describe her sister, "bubbly" would be it. Kelli would have made a great cheerleader. Today she was wearing her long, platinum blond hair in a ponytail that bounced up and down as she tried to get Leanna's attention.

"I see you, Kelli!" Leanna called. "Chill out!"

Shifting her duffel to her other shoulder, Leanna wove through the crowd to where her family was standing. Before she had a chance to say hello, Kelli threw her arms around Leanna in a crushing hug.

"I'm so glad you're home! It felt like you were gone for *years!*"

"I missed you, too," Leanna said. She hugged Kelli back. "I've got so much to tell you!"

"So do I!" Kelli exclaimed. "You know that beauty pageant I entered? Well—"

"Kelli, honey, save it for the car," Alison Van Haver interrupted gently. "Give me and dad a chance to say hi."

Kelli stepped back, and Leanna hugged her mother for the first time in two long months. Mrs. Van Haver was tall, with long, light blond hair. She wore casual cotton slacks and a plain T-shirt that matched her blue-gray eyes.

"You look so grown up," Mrs. Van Haver said, hugging Leanna tightly. "I hardly recognized my little girl."

Leanna wondered why her mother sounded almost tearful. She'd only been gone for two months! Stepping back, Leanna lifted her chin and straightened her shoulders. "Do you think I grew?" she asked hopefully.

Leanna's stepfather laughed. "No, sweetie, you're still the same Midget."

"Dad!" Leanna cried indignantly. He hadn't called her that embarrassing nickname in years!

Mr. Van Haver bent down to kiss Leanna's cheek, then slung her duffel bag over his shoulder.

"Careful, it's heavy," Leanna warned.

Her stepfather was tall and thin. Between his job as a librarian and his severe allergies, he didn't get outside much to exercise.

"Where's Scott?" Leanna asked Kelli as they stepped on the escalator to ride down to the baggage claim area. Mr. and Mrs. Van Haver were a few stairs below the girls.

Kelli shrugged. "You know Scott. He was all set to come, when his friend—that really old guy, what's his name?"

"Mr. Mancuso?" Leanna asked. At ninety-three,

Mr. Mancuso was the only one of Scott's friends who qualified as "really old." He'd been a cameraman during the early days of Hollywood, and Scott was making a documentary about his life.

"Yeah, Mancuso. Anyway, he remembered some stuff and wanted to tell Scott about it. So Scott ran to get it on tape before Mr. Mancuso forgot again," Kelli explained. "Scott said to tell you he's sorry and he'll call you tonight."

Leanna sighed. "I'm not surprised. When Scott's filming something, he barely remembers to eat, so I guess meeting his girlfriend's plane is too much to think about."

"Are you mad?" Kelli asked as they stepped off the escalator.

"No, not really," Leanna said.

During the forty-minute drive to Fair Oaks, Leanna told her family about Carlos and the boys, Dora's cooking, and their trip to Disneyland. The only thing she left out was Miguel. She could hardly wait to get Kelli alone and tell her all the juicy details.

Leanna's chance came after lunch, when she went upstairs to her bedroom to unpack. Kelli followed, offering to help. Leanna just shook her head. She'd seen the way Kelli "unpacked" after vacations. She usually dumped everything into the nearest drawer, and what didn't fit got tossed onto the floor of her closet.

Kelli went to her own room and came back with

a bottle of hot-pink nail polish. She kicked off her sandals and hopped onto Leanna's bed.

"Okay, we've heard the G-rated version, now tell me the good stuff." Kelli uncapped a bottle of bright pink polish and pulled out the brush. "Did you meet any hot guys in San Diego?"

"Just one, and he was really special." Leanna unzipped her duffel bag and began transferring the contents to her drawers. "He was so cute—"

"Got any pictures?" Kelli asked, painting her left thumb in bright pink.

Leanna shook her head. "No. I only met him yesterday, and I'd used up my last roll of film at Disneyland. Carlos and Dora took me to the Philippine Festival." Leanna rolled her eyes. "It was supposed to be this big surprise. Teach me about the Philippines. As if Carlos hadn't been jamming it down my throat all summer."

Kelli nodded. "I got your letter. All that disgusting stuff they made you eat! How did you stand it?"

"It wasn't all bad," Leanna said. She'd written to Kelli after Dora had served something called *dinuguan*, which looked like chocolate but turned out to be a stew made out of pig's blood. She'd eaten a few spoonfuls before Carlos had told her what it was. She'd been angry at the Maligs, and her letter to Kelli had made the *dinuguan* sound way grosser than it was.

"Anyway, surprise, surprise, I actually enjoyed the festival. Look what Carlos bought me." Leanna unzipped her garment bag and pulled out the yellow *terno* dress.

"It's gorgeous. Look at the cute sleeves!" Kelli pinched the fabric of one sleeve between her fingers. "What's this material? It doesn't feel like cotton."

"Pineapple fiber," Leanna said. "Cool, huh?"

"Yeah," Kelli agreed. "But there's a grass stain on the bottom."

Leanna lifted a handful of fabric. The yellow skirt had a green streak across the back.

"Oh, no. I hope it'll wash out," she said. "It must have happened when Miguel and I were sitting on the grass."

"Aha! Is he the cute guy you met?" Kelli asked.

Leanna nodded. "Yeah. Miguel and I walked around the festival together. We even watched a mock Philippine wedding."

"Sounds romantic." Kelli leaned back against Leanna's pillow, closed the bottle of nail polish, and shook it with her right hand. "Is that why you were rolling around on the grass with him?"

"We weren't rolling around! We were just sitting." Heat rushed to Leanna's cheeks as she remembered that Miguel had done more than just sit. "Okay, he kissed me," she blurted out, although Kelli hadn't said another word.

"Sounds serious." Kelli blew on her wet nails. "So . . . are you going to see him again?"

"How?" Leanna asked. She shoved some T-shirts into a drawer and slammed it savagely. "Miguel won't wait around for Thanksgiving or Christmas or whenever I get down to Carlos's again.

I'd be stupid to start something with a guy in San Diego. Although, if I lived there all the time—"

"No way!" Kelli cried. "You can't do that!"

"I'm not planning to." Leanna turned toward Kelli in surprise. "I just said *if* I lived in San Diego. Miguel is so cute. But I live here, and I can't forget about Scott," she explained.

"That's true! And think of all you'd miss if you moved to your father's," Kelli said. "You already missed the Miss Cocoa-Tropic Tan Pageant. I bombed big time, but you might have won. Having a year-round tan is a big advantage in those suntan oil pageants."

"Oh, I forgot all about that pageant." Leanna couldn't see herself as a beauty queen; but then, she hadn't thought of modeling, either, until Kelli had convinced her to enroll at Bayside instead of public high school. Entering the pageant with Kelli would have been fun, but visiting Carlos had ruined that plan.

"You should have seen the girl who won," Kelli went on. "She wore a slinky gold gown with rhinestone spaghetti straps. You know the white taffeta dress I bought? Huge mistake! I should have worn something with sequins. I swear, those judges just picked the fanciest dress, without even noticing who was inside it. A lot of other contestants thought so, too. Hey, want to see the tape? I've got a copy downstairs."

"But I haven't finished unpacking," Leanna protested. She wondered why Kelli was so excited about the pageant all of a sudden. It wasn't like Kelli to start talking about herself when they were talking about a major hunk.

"I'll help you unpack later." Kelli jumped off the bed, careful not to smudge her wet nails. "You've got to see the tape. You won't believe some of the bathing suits."

Leanna let Kelli drag her out of the room, still talking about the other contestants' clothing and hairstyles.

Kelli turned on the VCR in the family room, and they settled back on the sofa to watch the tape. There was Kelli coming down the runway, her blond hair piled on her head in elaborate curls. Several other Bayside students were in the pageant, too. Leanna recognized her friends, Wendy and DeShaun. She almost didn't recognize Sara. In June, Sara had had long brown hair.

"When did Sara become a redhead?" Leanna asked, staring at her friend's unfamiliar short curls.

"Right after you left," Kelli replied. "You missed a lot this summer."

"So I missed Sara's new hairdo. I can see it tomorrow."

"No, you can't," Kelli said. "Last week she shaved her head."

Leanna stared at the screen. It wasn't that Sara's hair was so important, or even the beauty pageant. It was the realization that life in Fair Oaks had gone on without her.

Time wouldn't stand still for Miguel, either. Months from now, if he even remembered her, she'd be the girl who'd lied to him, who'd promised to call but never did.

If only she could be in two places at once! But she had to choose. There was room for only one guy at a time in Leanna's heart.

"Leanna!" Kelli's voice broke into her thoughts. "I asked if I could borrow your red tank top tomorrow!"

Leanna blinked. "Uh, sure. Can I watch the rest of this later?"

"Where are you going?" Kelli asked as Leanna got up from the sofa.

"I'm going to call Scott," Leanna said.

It had been too long since she'd spoken to her boyfriend. Leanna hoped that Scott's familiar voice would help banish the other voice from her mind. The one that whispered softly but insistently in Tagalog, "Until we meet again."

Chapter Seven

"**O**F COURSE I want to see you again."
Leanna leaned against the kitchen wall,
twisting the white phone cord around her forearm.
"But, Carlos—"

"Leanna," her father interrupted gently. "I don't
mean to nag, but it would mean a lot to me if you
could call me Pa. Or Papa. Calling parents by their
first names is disrespectful. It's not—"

"I know, I know," Leanna broke in. "It's not the
Filipino way." Leanna knew that kids in the
Philippines called their parents "Ma" and "Pa," but
she *couldn't* do it. It sounded like something a hill-
billy would say. "Papa" was even worse. So babyish!

"So . . . are you coming to visit on Thanksgiving?" Carlos asked.

Kelli appeared in the kitchen doorway, wearing
a long-sleeved black wool dress and black suede

boots. Her outfit was much too heavy for the middle of autumn, but Leanna knew Kelli would have worn a fur coat if she thought it would please her date, Glenn Garrick.

"Thanksgiving's no good," Leanna said. "Grandma Van Haver's throwing a big party. The whole family has to come, whether we want to or not."

In the doorway, Kelli gestured frantically for Leanna to hang up.

Leanna put her hand over the mouthpiece. "Five minutes," she told Kelli.

"Glenn says we'll be late for the movie," Kelli scoffed.

"Five minutes," Leanna repeated, holding up five fingers of her left hand.

Kelli walked away, and Leanna focused on what Carlos was saying.

"I understand that the Van Havers are important." Carlos sounded a little sad. "But I'm your father. I'd like to be part of your life, too."

"I'd like that," Leanna said. "But I can't let Grandma down."

"How about another weekend? It doesn't have to be a holiday."

"I'll have to ask Mom," Leanna said. Not that her mother would object, but Carlos didn't need to know that. Using Mom as an excuse was easier than trying to explain how torn Leanna felt between her two families.

"Okay. Call me after you talk to her," Carlos

said. "The boys really miss you. Have you been practicing your Tagalog?"

Leanna rolled her eyes. The Tagalog tapes Carlos had given her were someplace in her bedroom, she wasn't sure where. She hadn't played them even once.

"I've got to go, Carlos," Leanna said. "My friends are waiting."

"I understand," Carlos replied.

Hanging up the phone, Leanna grabbed her purse from the back of a chair and headed for the family room. Scott was there, waiting with Kelli and Glenn.

As Leanna walked through the door, Glenn was talking about his favorite subject: himself.

"I *should* have been in that jeans commercial," Glenn told Kelli, who sat beside him on the love seat. She was gazing up at him like an adoring puppy. "But I didn't even get the audition. I'll bet my agent's sorry now. He sent Eddie Alvarez instead. Eddie flubbed his lines and got the old 'Don't call us, we'll call you.' If that agent had any brains, he'd have sent me. I could have made him *and* Bayside look good."

And if there's one thing Glenn's an expert on, it's looking good, Leanna thought. He was Bayside Academy's star male model, and he treated the Bayside girls like his personal harem.

Tonight, Glenn wore an olive T-shirt and a khaki fatigue jacket. His camouflage pants were tucked into lace-up combat boots. On anyone else, the outfit would have looked casual. But Glenn's boots were polished to a gleaming shine, and his clothes were crisply ironed. Glenn bragged that he didn't do housework; his mother waited on him hand and foot. Leanna wondered if his mother had also ironed the two precise waves in Glenn's light brown hair.

"Hi, Leanna." Glenn broke off his story to flash a smile that would have turned most Bayside girls to jelly. Leanna might have admired Glenn's smile, too, if he hadn't told everyone, over and over, how much money his parents had paid for his orthodontic work.

"You look nice," Glenn continued. His eyes roamed over Leanna's black leggings and bright tropical print blouse. "But I like my women in skirts."

"Good thing I'm not your *woman*," Leanna snapped. She already regretted this double date, and they hadn't even left the house!

Kelli, looking nervous, glanced from Glenn to Leanna. "Come on, you guys. We'll miss the movie."

At the word "movie," Scott's head snapped up. For the first time, he seemed to realize he wasn't alone in the room.

"Hey, yeah, we'd better get moving." Scott stood up, his long legs unfolding like a ladder. He was wearing one of his vintage outfits, a pair of black pleated slacks with a gray silk shirt and a pinstriped vest. His clothes themselves were dressier than Glenn's, but they were casually rumpled, with the sleeves pushed up past Scott's elbows.

Kelli and Glenn headed out to Glenn's van, but Leanna caught Scott's arm, holding him back. In a low voice, she asked, "Did you hear what that loser said to me?"

Scott blinked. "Of course not. I never listen to Glenn."

"He said he likes his women to wear skirts!" Leanna snapped. "And he looked at me like he expected me to run upstairs and change!"

"Why make a big deal out of it?" Scott asked mildly. "Glenn's harmless. Just ignore him."

Leanna shrugged and followed Scott out to Glenn's van. Scott was right. There was no point in starting an argument over Glenn's ignorant remark.

When they got to the Cinedome, Glenn insisted on driving around the parking lot to find the safest place to park his customized van. When they finally reached the ticket window, the movie they'd planned to see was already sold out.

"This is all your fault, Leanna." Glenn's eyes narrowed. "You stayed on the phone too long."

"Well, excuse me, Your Highness!" Leanna had had enough of Glenn's attitude. "I wasn't the one who drove around the parking lot all night."

"Chill out, you two," Scott said, stepping between Glenn and Leanna. "There are six movies playing here. Let's just pick another one."

Glenn darted a quick glance at the marquee.

"You've got to be kidding. They're all sissy movies, except *Hard Justice*."

"No way!" Leanna burst out. "I'm not watching some macho idiot blow up buildings for two hours."

Scott squeezed her hand. Not because he loved her, Leanna realized, but because he wanted her to shut up.

"I'm sure we can find something we'll all like," Scott said calmly. "How about *Falling for You*? It's a romantic comedy starring—"

"Those lovey-dovey films are for girls," Glenn interrupted. "Either we see *Hard Justice*, or I'm leaving."

Kelli leaned close to Leanna and whispered, "Try to get along with Glenn. *Please*." In a louder voice, she added, "*Hard Justice* sounds great, Glenn."

Scott tried to hold Leanna's hand as they walked into the lobby, but she angrily pulled away. Leanna was mad at everyone: Scott, Glenn, Kelli, even herself. Now she was doomed to watch a loud, violent film because she hadn't stood up for herself. She and Scott should have bought tickets for *Falling for You*, and let Glenn and Kelli see *Hard Justice*. But it was too late now.

After moving past the usher who tore their ticket stubs, Glenn and Kelli headed directly toward the snack bar. Sniffing the buttery popcorn aroma, Leanna felt her spirits lift slightly. Maybe the evening wouldn't be a *total* loss. Some hot buttered popcorn, an ice-cold lemonade, and a bag of Gummi Bears might improve her mood.

"Want some popcorn?" Scott must have read her thoughts.

Leanna started to say yes, but the word died on her lips as she caught sight of the guy behind the popcorn machine. Straight black hair framed a boyishly round face with dark brown almond-shaped eyes. Like the other theater employees, he wore a dorky red vest and a geeky bow tie with ugly white polyester slacks. But even in uniform, Leanna noticed his amazingly muscular arms, strong hands, and broad, solid chest.

Leanna wiped her damp palms on her dark leggings. She felt her heart pounding so loud, she was sure everyone could hear.

Miguel! she thought. *It has to be!* But how? Miguel lived in San Diego. How could he be working at a theater hundreds of miles from his home?

"Guess I asked a stupid question," Scott said, laughing. "Of course you want popcorn."

He turned to follow Kelli and Glenn toward the counter, but Leanna clutched his arm. "No, thanks! I don't want any."

Scott looked worried. "Why? Are you sick? You never sit through a movie without a ton of junk food."

"It's bad for my skin. I've got a fashion show coming up," Leanna said quickly, ducking behind Scott. She was thankful that his tall shoulders blocked her view of the refreshment stand. For once, Leanna was glad she was short. If that pop-corn guy really was Miguel, she didn't want him to see her with Scott!

"But you never break out," Scott said.

Leanna faked a laugh. "There's always a first time. Why take chances?" Feeling conspicuous in her brightly flowered shirt, Leanna ducked farther into Scott's shadow.

"What's really going on, Leanna?" Scott lowered his voice.

She had to get out of there—fast! Before her knees collapsed, or her heart burst from her chest. Before she did something crazy, like run over to the popcorn guy and throw her arms around him. Seeing Miguel again—if it really was Miguel—brought back all the excitement she'd felt during their first shy kiss. But what if Miguel found out about her lies . . . about Scott? Leanna would just die!

"I'm just not hungry," she told Scott. "It's no big deal. Come on, let's get inside before all the good seats are taken."

"But I thought you didn't care about *Hard Justice.*" Seeming bewildered, Scott let Leanna drag him toward the dark theater.

"If I have to see a bad movie, I don't want to get stuck behind some tall person with big hair," Leanna replied. She moved quickly toward the theater, glad it was dark enough to hide the blush on her face. If it was as red as it felt, she must have resembled a fire engine.

She knew she was being silly. That couldn't be

Miguel out there. And if by some miracle it was, he must have forgotten about her by now.

I've just got to find out if it's him, Leanna thought as she and Scott found seats near the back of the theater.

Scott touched her hand, and she almost screamed. "What's with you tonight?" he asked. "First you're too quiet, then you jump ten feet. Want to talk about it?"

Scott's sympathy made Leanna feel even worse. How could she even *think* about another guy, when Scott was so sweet?

"I'm fine," she said.

Scott started to say something, but then Glenn and Kelli appeared with a huge tub of popcorn. Leanna, who was sitting in the aisle seat, stood up to let them squeeze by. The popcorn smelled so good that Leanna's mouth watered.

"Want some?" Kelli asked, offering Leanna the bucket.

"No, thanks." Leanna couldn't accept. Not after making a big deal about refusing it to Scott.

Glenn dropped into the seat next to Scott. He began talking to Scott in a whisper loud enough for Leanna to hear. "Doesn't Leanna want popcorn? I can lend you some cash if you're running short, man."

Leanna couldn't hear Scott's reply, but then Glenn spoke again, even louder. "No way. Listen, I know how to make a girl happy. And I always give her what she wants."

Leanna shot Glenn a disgusted look. She couldn't believe what she was hearing. And then to top it off, Glenn dared to wink at her as the lights dimmed and the screen turned black. Glenn was actually flirting with her!

A moment later a noisy confusion of soldiers, tanks, and spurting blood shot across the screen. Just as Leanna was adjusting to the noise, a late-comer ran down the center aisle and slipped into the seat directly in front of her.

A tall blond woman whose hair was teased almost a foot high.

Leanna groaned. Great. The cotton candy hair in front of Leanna blocked her view of the lower part of the screen.

Leanna glanced at Scott. Macho action films weren't his favorite, but he was giving this one his undivided attention, as he did with every movie he saw. He liked studying special effects and camera angles. Leanna knew it would take an earthquake to pry him loose before the closing credits.

I should take a walk out to the lobby, Leanna thought. It couldn't hurt to just *look* at the popcorn guy. She wouldn't even have to talk to him. Just one quick look, to make sure he wasn't Miguel. Then she could relax and enjoy the rest of the night.

Leaning over, Leanna whispered in Scott's ear, "I'm going to the rest room. I'll be right back."

"Mmm-hmm," Scott murmured. His eyes were glued to the screen as a shirtless man with lots of tattoos aimed a flamethrower at a Jeep.

Leanna hurried up the center aisle. As long as the film kept running, Scott wouldn't notice if she were gone for five minutes or half an hour.

It would only take a second for her to stroll up to the snack bar and casually check the guy out.

Leanna closed her eyes and took a few deep breaths, the way her modeling teacher had taught her to relieve nervous tension. When she opened her eyes again, she felt a bit calmer.

But as she approached the snack bar, she could barely breathe. No one seemed to notice her, though. The three red-vested employees were all busy. A pudgy blond guy was ringing up an order on the cash register. A redheaded girl was handing an ice-cream bar to a little boy. And a third employee was bent over the counter.

Leanna caught her breath as she spied the name embroidered in gold thread on his tacky red vest. But she knew she didn't need to read it. His glossy dark hair and muscular arms spelled Miguel clearer than any alphabet.

He didn't look up. He scowled as he scrubbed the sticky counter with a sponge.

Run, Leanna thought. *Run back to the movie before he sees you!*

"Hi, Miguel."

Miguel's head snapped up at the sound of a strangely familiar female voice. He dropped the sponge onto the floor as he stared at the petite girl with loose, silky black hair standing at the counter.

Leanna! She looked just as pretty as she had that day in August at the Philippine Festival . . . and many times after, in his dreams.

Leanna Malig. He'd remember her name forever. And now she was standing at the counter, like an angel out of thin air. In that split second he remembered their magical kiss. The touch of her lips sending a warm glow throughout his body. Miguel had thought of Leanna often, but when his family had moved to Sacramento, he'd assumed he'd never see her again.

"Leanna!"

"You—you dropped your sponge." Leanna bent to retrieve it, then handed it to Miguel.

When their hands touched, Miguel felt a spark of electricity tingle between them. Leanna was really here. It wasn't a dream. "What are you doing here?" he asked.

Leanna didn't let go of the sponge. "I—I'm seeing a movie. What about you?"

"I'm cleaning the counter," Miguel replied, grinning. He removed the sponge from her hand, set it on the counter, and clasped her hand again. It felt much nicer without the wet sponge between them. "I can't believe you're here. So much has happened since I saw you at the festival. When I gave you my number, I had no idea I'd be moving, and—"

"Miguel," a shrill voice interrupted from behind him, "is that girl buying something?"

Miguel didn't have to turn around. He knew exactly who'd said that, and he could picture the smug look on her face. His coworker Danette didn't like Miguel and was always trying to get him in trouble.

He quickly dropped Leanna's hand. "I was just about to ask her," he said. "Miss, may I take your order?"

"I'll take her order," Danette said. "You go mop up that spill in the back room."

Miguel bit back an angry retort. The theater manager, Ms. Esquivel, had put Danette in charge that evening.

"I'll get right to it," Miguel told Danette in his most polite voice. He turned back to Leanna. "I can't talk now—"

"Come on already!" Danette shrieked. "Talking to friends when you're on duty is against the rules."

"Okay, okay." Miguel leaned toward Leanna and whispered, "I get off work at midnight. Can you meet me outside?"

Leanna seemed to hesitate, and Miguel held his breath. Finally she said, "Sure. I'll be here."

"Promise?" The word slipped out, and Miguel wished he could take it back. He wanted Leanna to think he was cool, not desperate.

But Leanna's perfect lips curved into a smile. Then she whispered, "I promise."

Danette shoved a mop into his hand. "Get to work, lover boy!"

Miguel whistled as he walked jauntily into the

back storeroom. He hardly noticed Tom's mean laughter or Danette's steely glare. For the second time, against all odds, fate had sent him this beautiful, old-fashioned girl of his dreams. And this time, he wasn't going to let her get away.

Chapter Eight

"**I** CAN'T BELIEVE you're sneaking out." Kelli planted herself in front of Leanna's bedroom door and folded her arms. She might have looked stern if she hadn't been wearing baby-doll pajamas with teddy bears printed all over them.

"Quiet! You'll wake Mom and Dad." Leanna sank down on her bed and glanced at her watch. She needed to be out of there in five minutes if she wanted to keep her promise to Miguel.

Kelli leaned against the closed door. "You know we're not allowed out after midnight. And if Dad finds out you took his car without permission, you'll be grounded until you're too old to date."

"He won't find out. I'll be right back." Leanna looked pleadingly at her stepsister. "I'd wake Dad up and ask, only I'm in a big hurry—"

"And you know he'd say no," Kelli broke in.

"You already had one date tonight. I doubt Dad would let you go on another."

"This isn't a date," Leanna snapped. "I'm just going to talk to him."

"How does Scott feel about you *talking* to this guy?" Kelli demanded.

"Since when do *you* have a problem with dating two guys at once?"

Kelli's face flushed. "We're not talking about me," she said, tossing back her silvery blond hair. "And anyway, none of those guys meant anything to me."

"Not even Glenn?" Leanna asked softly.

"Glenn turned out to be the biggest loser of all." Kelli collapsed into a sitting position, still blocking the door. "I saw him flirting with you. What a slimeball!"

Kelli sniffled. Leanna grabbed a box of tissues from the dresser and handed it to her.

"Thanks." Kelli wiped her nose and took a deep breath. "Listen, Leanna, you don't know how lucky you are to have someone like Scott. He's the only guy at Bayside who's not totally into himself. He really cares about you. Why would you risk that for some guy you hardly know?"

"Maybe you're right," Leanna said slowly. She sat down on the floor near her stepsister. Scott *was* nice, and she didn't want to hurt him. But the butterflies in her stomach didn't dance around like they did when she was around Miguel.

"You said Miguel's from the Philippines," Kelli

70

went on. "Aren't you setting yourself up for some major problems? Just think of Mom and Carlos. Or Dad and Leslie."

Leslie was Kelli's birth mother. As usual, when Kelli said "Leslie" she curled her lip as if saying "monster" or "wicked witch." Unlike Carlos Malig, Leslie Van Haver didn't call or write to her daughter. Leslie had left a five-month-old Kelli alone with her father. And that was the last time Kelli had seen her.

"If only Mom and Dad had gotten married right after high school instead of going to different colleges." Kelli sighed. She tossed her used tissue into the wastebasket. "It would have been so perfect. Dad wouldn't have met Leslie, and Mom wouldn't have met Carlos."

"And neither of us would have been born," Leanna pointed out.

"True, but think how much happier Mom and Dad would be. You know why their first marriages didn't work," Kelli reminded her. "Their differences were stronger than their love."

"But we're not our parents," Leanna said. She twisted a lock of hair around her finger.

"Right!" Kelli jumped to her feet, waving her arms excitedly. "We don't have to make the same mistakes our parents did. I know Miguel seems exciting and different, but he's *too* different. You're better off with someone like Scott."

Leanna forced herself to laugh. "Lighten up, Kelli! I'm just going to *see* Miguel, not marry him."

Kelli uncurled her legs and got up from the

71

floor. "Yeah, but *why* are you going to see him?" Kelli's eyes narrowed. "Are you going to tell Miguel about Scott?"

"I don't know." Leanna sighed.

Kelli moved away from the door. "You can tell him that kiss in San Diego was just a summer vacation thing."

"I'll think about it," Leanna promised. The truth was, she had no idea what she would say to Miguel. She only knew that she had to see him again.

"Well, don't be long," Kelli warned as Leanna pushed open the bedroom door. "And be careful with Dad's car."

Leanna tiptoed down the dark stairs and into the kitchen. Without turning on the light, she reached for Dad's car keys on the hook by the telephone. Mom always kept her keys in her purse, but Dad left his hanging where anyone could get them. Sometimes he left cash lying around, too. He had this theory that if you showed your kids that you trusted them, they'd live up to your expectations.

Leanna hated to betray his trust, but there was no other way. As Kelli had pointed out, asking to use the car was out of the question. Dad would definitely say no, and he'd probably add that if Miguel wanted to see her, he should come by the house in the daytime and meet him and her mom.

Leanna could just see herself explaining, "Well, uh, Dad, Miguel thinks Carlos and Dora are my parents." Dad would definitely take *that* the wrong way.

Quietly, Leanna slipped through the door to the garage and flipped on the overhead light. She looked at her watch and stifled a groan. Great! She'd have to hit all green lights to make it to the Cinedome before Miguel left. She didn't want him to think she'd stood him up.

This isn't a date, Leanna reminded herself as she unlocked her stepfather's white Volvo and slid behind the wheel.

Leanna pressed the automatic garage-door opener, and the aluminum door lifted slowly. The clanging, which Leanna barely noticed in the daytime, sounded like a million ghosts rattling their chains. Leanna could see nothing outside the garage but a square of inky darkness.

For a split second, she thought about closing the garage door, going back upstairs, and forgetting all about seeing Miguel.

But she'd promised. She owed it to him to show up, even if it was just to tell him that their two worlds could never meet. Leanna turned the key in the ignition. The engine roared to life, and the headlights pierced the darkness like searchlights on a police helicopter.

Nearly panicking, Leanna floored the accelerator and sped up the driveway before she lost her nerve.

Miguel shifted position on the stone bench outside the Cinedome entrance. From here, he had a good view of the empty parking lot. He checked his watch again. It was 12:15.

She'll be here, he told himself. But what if her parents hadn't let her go out? He was so used to getting off work at midnight that he sometimes forgot how late it really was, especially for someone with strict parents.

Miguel frowned, checking his watch again. Why hadn't he known Leanna's parents wouldn't let her meet a strange boy after midnight? He hadn't been thinking clearly at all.

I should have met her parents, he told himself. *Spent some time with her family before meeting her alone.*

Miguel had just decided to give up and go home when a white Volvo screeched into a space close to the building. Leanna got out and walked toward the theater, looking from left to right as she crossed the pavement. In the glow of the streetlights, Miguel saw that she wore the same red-flowered blouse and black leggings she'd had on earlier, only this time she'd thrown a jean jacket over her shoulders.

He stood up so she could see him. "Leanna, over here."

Leanna spotted Miguel near the theater entrance. He was still wearing the dorky red vest, white shirt, and white trousers he'd had on earlier. As she got closer, she saw that his pants were stained with chocolate. Or maybe cola.

As she approached, Leanna wasn't sure if she was glad or sorry that he hadn't given up and gone home. She still had no idea what she was going to say to him.

"Sorry I'm late," she began.

"No problem." Miguel smiled at her, and for a moment Leanna thought that even if Dad grounded her for life for taking the car, it was worth it to see Miguel's smile again.

"Let's go somewhere and talk," Miguel said. "There's an all-night diner up the street."

"I can't." If she went to a diner with Miguel, it would definitely be a date. Leanna didn't want to go out with Miguel until she'd had a chance to break up with Scott. Besides, she had to get the car back before Dad noticed that it—and she—were missing.

"I don't have much time. I have to be home soon." Leanna sat down on a nearby bench. "We can talk right here."

"Okay." Miguel sat down next to her.

Leanna felt the warmth of his skin through her jean jacket as their shoulders touched on the narrow bench. She caught the pleasant scent of his spicy aftershave, mixed with the faint but unmistakable aroma of buttered popcorn.

"So . . . what are you doing in Sacramento?" Leanna asked. "Besides selling popcorn, I mean."

"I live here now," he said. "It happened pretty fast. I know I told you my parents worked at Luzon Gardens Restaurant."

Leanna nodded. "I remember your mother's *lumpia*. It was the best!"

"Well, lots of other people thought so, too. A man named Mr. Nuñez was at the festival," Miguel explained. "He was all set for the grand opening of his restaurant up here when his head chef quit. He went to the festival in search of a replacement, and he offered the job to both my parents. My parents had been thinking of moving up here, anyway—my dad's brother lives here. We moved a few weeks ago."

"How great for your parents!" Leanna exclaimed. "You must have been bummed, though. Changing schools, leaving all your friends . . ."

"I'd just met you, so I wasn't in any hurry to move," Miguel shrugged. "I thought I'd never see you again once we got here. But I had to come with my parents."

Leanna remembered Carlos telling her that the three most important things in the Philippine culture were family, religion, and education. Hanging out with friends didn't even make the top ten.

"So when can I meet your family?" Miguel asked, leaning even closer to her. "I can't wait to see your brother Toby again. And I want to have a long talk with your father. Once he meets me, I just know he'll give me permission to go out with you."

"No!" Leanna blurted out.

Miguel drew back sharply, looking hurt. "I thought there was something special between us at the festival. But if you don't want to go out with me, well . . ."

"That's not it. I do want to go out with you!" Leanna cried, clutching his arm. She looked down at her hand, wrapped around Miguel's tanned forearm. She'd come here to say good-bye to Miguel, and here she was practically begging him to stay!

Letting go of his arm, Leanna nervously raked her fingers through her long hair. "I want to go out with you, but you can't ask my parents. They're not here."

"What do you mean?" Miguel asked. "Are they all right? I hope nothing's happened to them!"

Leanna stared at him. Then she took a deep breath and hoped her voice wouldn't shake. "My parents are fine," she said. "They're still in San Diego. I'm here by myself because I won a scholarship to a really great private school in Fair Oaks. That's a few miles from here."

"You must really miss your parents," Miguel said. "How awful for you."

"It's not so bad. I mean, I miss them," she said hastily, "but Bayside's a good school. And it's really hard to get into. All the classes had been filled for the fall semester, but there was a cancellation at the last minute, so I got the spot."

Miguel nodded. "When my brother Noriel was ready for college, he came to America. We all missed him, but we wanted him to have the best education. So I understand how it is."

Her plan was working!

"My father went to college in California," she told Miguel. "Then he went back to the Philippines. And now he teaches junior high in San Diego."

"I thought you said you'd never been to the Philippines," Miguel said, raising his eyebrows.

"I haven't! My, uh—*pa* only went back there for a *short* time. Two weeks," Leanna said. "To visit his parents. The rest of us stayed home."

Miguel nodded. "So, do you have other relatives in California?"

"No. None." Leanna fell silent, hoping Miguel wouldn't ask any more questions about her family.

"Then where are you living?"

"In—in Fair Oaks." Leanna's heart began pounding again. Now what could she say? She couldn't tell him she had her own apartment; she was way too young for that.

Suddenly she remembered Hiroko Yamasaki, an exchange student who'd lived with her friend Wendy's family last year. Hiroko was from an old-fashioned, overprotective Japanese family. And they didn't seem to mind her living with—what had Wendy called it? A host family.

"I live with Mr. and Mrs. Van Haver and their daughter, Kelli. They're my host family," Leanna explained. "They look after me and all, but I'm not related to them."

"Then I guess I'll have to talk to Mr. Van Haver, then," Miguel said, as if it were all settled. "Will he be home tomorrow? I could come by in the afternoon, before work."

"Yeah, I think he'll be around," Leanna said. Actually, both her parents were going to an antique show tomorrow afternoon. When Miguel showed up, she could tell him how sorry she was that he'd missed the Van Havers, but that before they left, they'd given her permission to go to the mall or wherever Miguel wanted to go. It could work!

"Here's my address and phone number," she said as she searched through her jean jacket for a pen and paper.

"Great. I'll come by around one tomorrow."

Perfect! By that time, the Van Havers would be safely at the antique show.

"See you tomorrow," Miguel said, walking her to her car. As Leanna opened the passenger door, he leaned over and brushed a quick kiss across her forehead. *"Mahal kita,* Leanna."

"What does that mean?" Leanna asked.

Miguel laughed. His eyes shined like black diamonds in the moonlight. "Someday, maybe, I'll tell you."

Leanna sang along to the romantic ballad playing on the radio as she drove home late that night. When she'd left the house, she'd had no idea how to explain the Van Havers to Miguel. But everything had worked out perfectly. With any luck, Miguel would never come face-to-face with her parents; and even if he did, Leanna could easily explain any minor problems that might come up. She could even say that her host parents preferred her to call them "Mom" and "Dad."

Leanna congratulated herself on her quick thinking. Now all she had to do was put Dad's car back in the garage and sneak upstairs without waking her family.

As she pulled into the driveway, Leanna realized that her luck had run out. Several windows in the house were lit up, including the kitchen and her parents' bedroom.

For a moment, Leanna considered throwing the car into reverse and peeling out of the driveway. Instead, she pressed the garage-door opener and drove slowly inside.

Leanna shifted into park. Before she could turn off the engine, the door to the house burst open. Her parents were standing there in their matching navy blue bathrobes, looking as if they were about to strangle Leanna with their bare hands.

Chapter Nine

"**K**ELLI, YOU'VE GOT to help me," Leanna begged the moment her parents left the house the next day. "Miguel will be here in an hour."

"No way!" Kelli grabbed a diet soda from the fridge and popped the top. "Aren't you in enough trouble for sneaking out last night? You heard what Mom and Dad said. You're grounded all week. That definitely means no guys at the house."

"But you owe me," Leanna said. She pushed her half-eaten tuna sandwich around on her plate. "You could have covered for me last night."

Kelli set her soda can down on the kitchen table. "Oh, right. Like, when Dad started yelling that someone was stealing the Volvo, I should have let him call the police. Then you could've gotten busted by the cops instead of Dad."

"Okay . . . I guess you had no choice," Leanna admitted.

Kelli sat down at the table across from Leanna. "Hey, are you going to finish your lunch? I'm starved."

Leanna took another bite, then pushed her sandwich away. "I don't have time. I've got to pull down all those family pictures in the hallway."

"Why?" Kelli asked, reaching for a potato chip.

"Because I'm in them! Miguel thinks Carlos and Dora are my parents. You guys are supposed to be my host family here in Fair Oaks," Leanna explained. "He thinks I just met you last month. How can I explain all those old pictures of the four of us?"

Without waiting for an answer, Leanna hurried to the hallway that connected the kitchen and living room. It was lined on both sides with framed photos, some from several years ago. There were even a couple of just Mom, Dad, and Leanna. Leanna grabbed those first. Miguel might not recognize Leanna as a toddler, but he was sure to wonder why the blond Van Havers were posing with a dark-skinned child.

Leanna's arms were loaded with pictures when Kelli came out of the kitchen. "I can't believe you're doing this," she said.

Leanna tucked one last photo under her arm and headed upstairs. "I'll put them back when Miguel leaves."

Kelli followed her up the steps. "Oh, so we're just not good enough for Miguel."

Leanna kicked open her bedroom door and

dumped the framed photos on her bed. "I never said that. I want you to meet Miguel, and eventually he'll meet Mom and Dad, too."

"Then why are you pretending we're your *host* family?" Kelli asked. "I thought you were going to tell him the truth."

"I will. Later." Leanna headed downstairs to get the rest of the pictures off the walls. Kelli followed, still trying to convince her to tell Miguel the truth.

"Kelli, Miguel can't handle the truth yet." Leanna had thought about it all last night— especially after her parents' lecture on trust and responsibility. "His family is supertraditional. His parents have been married forever. You should have seen his face when I told him I was living here without my mom and dad. He thought they had died or something. I guess in his mind, that's the only good excuse for not living with both your parents."

Leanna yanked a photo from the wall and thrust it into Kelli's hands. "Miguel's looking for a true-blue Filipina. He thinks *I'm* one-hundred percent Filipina."

"Then why do you think Miguel's so great?" Kelli asked. "He sounds prejudiced."

"Well . . . ," Leanna said as they started upstairs, carrying the rest of the family photos. "What if you met a really hot guy, and he said, 'Hi, my name's Jake, and I just spent five years in jail for robbing a liquor store.' Would you go out with him?"

"That's a dumb question." Kelli shook her head,

83

looking disgusted. "Maybe I've had a few lousy boyfriends, but I don't date criminals."

"Okay." Leanna dropped the family photos on her bed with the others. "Now, say you meet this guy who's smart, gorgeous, and wonderful in every way. You go out with him for a few months, and you're totally in love. He makes your knees weak whenever you're with him. He thinks you're the nicest, most beautiful girl he's ever known. You trust him completely—"

"Lead me to him," Kelli broke in. "He sounds perfect!"

Leanna nodded. "He is, except for one thing. After you've been dating awhile, he tells you he was arrested once for shoplifting. He and a bunch of his junior high friends dared each other and he got caught. Would you dump him?"

"I guess not," Kelli said. "If it had just been an innocent dare gone bad . . . and he knew it was wrong. . . . And besides, I'm already crazy in love with him."

"See?" Leanna interrupted. "Now you understand why I can't tell Miguel the truth yet. If I tell him about you and Mom and Dad, he won't want to go out with me. But if he gets to know me and my so-called host family first, he'll like us so much that when I *do* tell him the truth, he won't have a major problem with it. He'll even forgive me for lying. He'll see that I *had* to lie, because it was the only way we could get together."

Kelli shook her head. "You're crazy if you think

I'll help you with this lame setup. I'm outta here. I have to get ready for a shoot, and you're supposed to mow the lawn this afternoon."

"Kelli, please! It'll only take you a few minutes." Leanna gestured toward the family photos on her bed. "Can you stick some other pictures in these frames, then put them back on the walls? I don't want Miguel to notice the empty hooks on the walls."

"Where am I going to get fifteen eight-by-tens?" Kelli asked. "And why don't you do it yourself?"

"I have to mow the lawn." Leanna pulled her hair over her right shoulder and began twisting it into a braid. "If I hurry, I can finish before Miguel shows up. As long as the grass is mowed, Mom and Dad won't suspect a thing."

Leanna fastened her braid with an elastic and turned to Kelli, who was gazing at one of the family photos with an uncertain expression.

"Please!" Leanna begged. "I've helped you impress guys. Remember that guy in fifth grade with the worm collection? I dug up Mom's whole vegetable garden so you could have a worm collection, too."

"Okay, okay. I'll do it," Kelli said, shuddering. "Just don't mention creepy Gene Quigley or his worms again! And another thing—if Mom and Dad catch Miguel over here, I had nothing to do with it!"

"Thanks, Kelli." Leanna gave her stepsister a quick hug. She was nervous about disobeying her parents again, but this time her plan was foolproof. The antique show her parents went to closed at five, and they loved looking at old furniture. No way would they be home before the show ended. She had the entire afternoon!

Miguel drove his ancient station wagon slowly down the street, checking the numbers on every mailbox he passed. He braked beside a driveway lined with forsythia bushes and leaned out the window to see the box hidden by the slender green branches. Yes, this was the address Leanna had given him, and the nameplate below it read Van Haver.

Miguel turned into the driveway. There were no other cars parked in it, so he pulled all the way up to the closed garage door.

As he climbed from the ugly brown car, Miguel looked at the two-story house Leanna shared with the Van Havers. It was similar to the one his family rented. The average-sized lawn was freshly mown, and the hum coming from behind the weathered redwood fence told him that someone was mowing the backyard.

Clutching the bouquet of yellow roses he'd bought for Leanna, Miguel approached the front door. A large orange and white cat sprawled on its side and blocked the path. Most of its left ear was missing. The cat yawned, and Miguel saw that the cat was missing several teeth as well.

"Hi, fella." Miguel stooped to scratch behind the cat's only ear. It closed its eyes and nudged its head against his palm, purring softly.

"See you later." Miguel gave the cat a final pat,

then stepped over its sprawled body and rang the doorbell.

Several seconds passed, but no one answered. Miguel pressed the bell again. If no one came this time, he'd call over the back fence to whomever was mowing the lawn.

Suddenly the door flew open. "You must be Miguel," said a loud girl's voice. "I'm Kelli Van Haver. Come on in."

Miguel couldn't help staring. The girl in the doorway was much taller than he, and her black high-heeled sandals increased her height by another three inches. Her long, silvery blond hair was piled on her head in an elaborate arrangement of braids and ringlets. She wore a strapless black and white dress, with rhinestones sparkling on her ears. And she had a ton of makeup on her face. *Way* too much, even for the fancy outfit.

For a moment, Miguel wasn't even sure if Kelli Van Haver was pretty or not. She was dazzling . . . but in an overdone way. If this was what she wore to hang around her house on a Saturday afternoon, he was afraid to know what she thought of his casual jean shorts and T-shirt.

As Miguel hesitated in the doorway, the cat's soft bulk brushed past his legs and sprang through the open door.

Kelli let out a piercing shriek. "Tumbleweed! Get out of here, you big ugly hair ball!"

Miguel couldn't believe a girl would talk that way to her own cat.

"Great, he got away," Kelli muttered. "Wait till I get my hands on that cat. I'll strangle him."

Miguel stepped awkwardly into the entrance hall. "Is Leanna home?"

"She's finishing up her chores," Kelli said, staring at the bouquet in Miguel's hand. "You can wait for her, but you'll have to leave those outside."

"Why? They're for Leanna," Miguel said sharply. He wanted to make a good impression on Leanna's host family, but he couldn't understand why Kelli was staring at the fragrant roses as if they were a bunch of weeds.

"Well, uh, I guess it won't hurt to bring them in," Kelli stammered. "Follow me."

Kelli turned smoothly on her heel and seemed to float down the hallway. Miguel followed her, wondering how she could walk so gracefully in such ridiculously high shoes.

As he walked down the hall, Miguel noticed the framed photos on both sides of the walls. It wasn't unusual to hang family photos; his mother had a bunch in their living room. But the Van Havers' photos were pretty strange.

For one thing, they were all of Kelli. Some were in color, others black and white, but all were close-ups of Kelli from either the waist up or just head shots. In some, her hair was teased and sprayed so that it looked like a wig. In all of them, Kelli's clothes looked like costumes: fur coats, black leather jackets, white feather boas.

Kelli led him into a small kitchen. "Have a

seat. Want me to put those roses in water?"

"No, thanks. I'd like to give them to Leanna before you put them in a vase." Miguel clutched the roses protectively as he sat down at the kitchen table.

"Leanna's mowing the lawn," Kelli explained. "Want something to drink? Iced tea, cola, root beer?"

"Iced tea sounds good." Miguel watched Kelli take a pitcher of tea from the fridge.

It seemed as if Kelli were trying to be friendly, but Miguel felt uncomfortable around her. After handing him the tea, she perched on the edge of her seat and watched him drink it. She didn't talk, and Miguel felt like some exotic animal in a zoo.

Miguel wished Kelli would leave, but instead she popped the top of a can of diet soda and took a sip. "So, Miguel," she asked, "how do you like Sacramento?"

"It's fine." It had actually been pretty dull until last night when he'd seen Leanna. But Kelli didn't need to know that. "Is your dad home?" Miguel asked. "I'd like to meet him."

"Nope, no one's home," Kelli said. She took a quick gulp of soda.

Miguel forced himself to smile at Kelli. "Is it okay if I go out back . . . help Leanna finish the lawn?"

"Great idea." Kelli looked relieved. "I've got to redo my makeup," she added. "Some of my lipstick rubbed off on my soda can."

Trust me, you've got plenty left, Miguel thought. But he kept smiling as Kelli pushed aside a curtain, revealing a sliding glass door. Through the glass, Miguel saw a huge backyard. Leanna, wearing jade green shorts and a matching green and white tee, was pushing a massive lawn mower.

Dropping his flowers on the table, Miguel pushed open the door. The sight of petite Leanna wrestling with the heavy mower was more than he could bear.

As he stepped through the door, a loud sneeze exploded behind him. "For heaven's sake, shut that door!" Kelli yelled. Before he could obey, Kelli herself yanked the glass door closed. Miguel was surprised she didn't give him a hard shove while she was at it.

He cupped his hands and shouted over the mower's roar, "Hey, Leanna! Need some help?"

Leanna turned off the mower and walked over to him. Her hair, in a single braid reaching nearly to the hem of her shorts, glistened with perspiration, and her cheeks were pink from the heat. Even though she looked ready to drop from exhaustion, she was smiling.

"Don't get too close," she said, stopping several feet away. "I'm pretty sweaty."

"I don't mind if you don't."

She stepped into his arms, and he hugged her close. Her heart, beating against his chest, felt like part of his own. "I don't care how sweaty you are, I'd rather hold you than someone like Kelli, who's all perfume and lip gloss and nothing else."

Leanna laughed. "That's sweet. Strange, but sweet."

Reluctantly, he let her go. "Let's get this yard finished so we can get out of here."

While Miguel finished mowing, Leanna raked the clippings into piles. When he finished the last strip of lawn, he helped her gather the clippings into garbage bags.

"Hey, Miguel," Leanna said.

He turned, and something soft exploded against his chest. Leanna giggled and stooped down for another handful of grass.

"Hey!" he yelled.

Leanna flung another grass ball at his head. "Got you!" she shouted.

Miguel brushed clippings from his hair. "Okay, if it's a fight you want, you're gonna get it."

"Not if I get you first!"

Picking up a handful of grass, Miguel chased her around a tree. Leanna dodged his throw and ran back for more ammunition.

"No fair!" he hollered as he watched Leanna pick up an entire bag of clippings. "What do you think you're doing with that?"

"Just watch!"

Smiling wickedly, Leanna walked toward him with the bag. Miguel waited until she was close enough, and then, just as she tipped the bag over his head, he grabbed the opposite side and pushed it in her direction.

Leanna wrestled it away and lost her balance. Miguel grabbed her around the waist, but he skidded on the plastic garbage bag. Shrieking with laughter, they tumbled to the ground together. Grass clippings tickled their necks and tangled in their hair and clothing.

"I didn't know you were such a wild woman." Miguel got to his feet, pulling Leanna up with him. "I can't believe we have to rake all over again."

"I don't care." Leanna put her arms around his neck. "You were looking so serious, I had to do something to make you smile."

Miguel rested his forehead against hers. He liked the fact that they were nearly the same height. Without any effort, he could gaze into her eyes. And if he tilted his head just a bit, their lips would touch.

"Leanna," he said huskily. "I know another way you can make me smile."

"Oh, yeah?" Leanna's dark eyes flashed teasingly. "Is this some strange Philippine custom I don't know about?"

Miguel's arms tightened around her waist. "I promise you'll know about this."

Slowly, as if drawn by some magnetic force, Miguel's lips met hers. His eyes closed, and suddenly, it was as if the past few weeks had never happened. He and Leanna were back at the Philippine Festival in San Diego, only this time their kiss was neither shy nor hesitant, but deep and full of promise. Leanna was in his arms, and nothing else mattered.

When Miguel finally opened his eyes, Leanna

was smiling at him. Her face was flushed, and grass sprinkled her hair like green dandruff. She was beautiful. And as her soft hand moved up to touch his cheek, she made him feel like the most important guy in the world.

He kissed her again. Her lips were warm, and she tasted faintly of new-mown grass. Time seemed to stand still as they held each other.

"Oh, no," Leanna said, breaking away from him.

"What's wrong?" he asked, feeling hurt and confused. But then he saw Leanna looking over his shoulder at the house.

"I'm in major trouble," Leanna moaned.

Chapter Ten

LEANNA HAD NEVER been so embarrassed in her life. One minute, she was kissing Miguel, forgetting that they weren't the only two people on the planet. The next minute, her parents were *watching* her kiss Miguel.

"Boy, they look ready to blow," Miguel said. "Didn't you tell them I was coming over?"

"Uh—yeah," Leanna stammered, her knees going weak. Miguel's strong arm around her waist was the only sturdy thing holding her up. A good Filipina would never sneak around with a boy behind her parents'—or host parents'—backs!

"It's the lawn," she said. "I promised to finish it before they got home."

"I'll tell them it's my fault," Miguel said.

Leanna shook her head. "No, I'll handle it." She was flattered that Miguel wanted to rescue her. But the less he spoke to her parents, the better. Maybe she could still pull this off. Mrs. Van Haver slid open the glass door. "Leanna," she called, "could you come here, please?"

Her mother's voice was cool and controlled, but Leanna wasn't fooled. Mrs. Van Haver always sounded her calmest when handing out particularly awful punishments.

"I'll be right back," Leanna told Miguel. She slowly walked over to the sliding glass door.

Her mother stood in the open doorway. Her dad was still on the other side of the room, where it was safe. He and Kelli were violently allergic to fresh-cut grass.

"Here." Mrs. Van Haver reached behind her and, to Leanna's astonishment, handed her a gorgeous bouquet of yellow roses.

"They're beautiful," Leanna said with a puzzled frown. She took the bouquet from her mother. Why was Mom giving her flowers instead of punishing her? "But Dad's allergic to roses."

"No kidding," Mr. Van Haver said from inside the house. Leanna looked past her mother and saw that her stepdad's eyes were beginning to water.

"I assume they're from that boy outside," Leanna's mother said. "Go outside and thank him. Tell him about your dad's allergies, and then ask him to go home."

"But he brought me flowers," Leanna said in awe. "I can't just give back the roses and tell him to get lost! That would be rude."

96

Her mother's expression didn't soften a bit. "You can call him later. Who is he, anyway? I've never seen him before."

"His name is Miguel Sarmiento. I met him in San Diego. He just moved here, and he doesn't know anyone. I know I'm grounded," Leanna went on, "but couldn't you *please* make this one exception?"

"He looks like a nice young man," Mrs. Van Haver admitted as she looked outside.

Leanna followed her mother's gaze and saw that Miguel was raking the spilled grass clippings. For a moment, she thought her mother might weaken. Then her heart sank as Mrs. Van Haver folded her arms.

"But you sneaked out last night, and now you have a friend over when you're grounded," Mrs. Van Haver said, shaking her head. "I'm sorry, but Miguel has to leave."

"Tell him I'll welcome him with open arms when he isn't covered with grass clippings," Mr. Van Haver added. He blew his nose with a loud honk. "Take him through the gate, not through the house. Unless you don't mind lying awake all night listening to Kelli and me sneeze."

Mrs. Van Haver ended the conversation by shutting the glass door, but Leanna had a feeling their discussion was far from over. She walked over to Miguel, who was still busy raking. His face fell when she handed him the roses.

"Mr. Van Haver is allergic to them," Leanna

97

explained. "I'm sorry, but I have to ask you to leave."

Miguel dropped the rake. "Just because I brought you the wrong kind of flowers?" He shook his head, looking disgusted. "Leanna, maybe it's none of my business, but your host family seems pretty weird."

"Come on. Let's talk about it out front." Leanna glanced nervously toward the sliding door. Her mother was still standing there, watching to see that she obeyed. Dad was gone, probably taking one of his allergy pills.

As they walked through the gate and around the side of the house, Leanna tried to catch Miguel's eye. But he just stared at the ground. His lips were pressed together, and he shook his head again.

An ugly station wagon stood in the driveway. It was incredibly old, and mostly brown except for one blue door. Miguel marched over to it, yanked open the blue door, and hurled the roses across the front seat.

Leanna cleared her throat. "Miguel, please don't be mad. I don't want to break our date, but I have to do what the Van Havers say. Right now that means finishing the yard by myself and—and not seeing you for a week. It's like last night when you were on duty. You wanted to talk to me, but you had to mop the floor."

"It's not the same." Miguel's hands gripped her shoulders. "I don't live with my boss, and she doesn't tell me who I can or can't date! What do your parents think of the way the Van Havers treat you?"

"They—they think it's okay," Leanna stammered. "I mean, I ought to do something to earn my room and board."

"But you're not their servant! Can't Mr. Van Haver mow his own lawn?"

"He's allergic to grass, too," Leanna said.

Suddenly the front door of the house burst open. Kelli, dressed in her fancy black and white dress, stepped outside, holding the neighbors' cat by the scruff of his neck.

"Get out!" she shrieked, tossing the cat on the lawn. "And stay out!"

"Did you see that?" Miguel's lip curled in disgust. "She's abusing an innocent animal."

"That's not her cat. Tumbleweed belongs to the neighbors, but he thinks this house is a giant litter box. He's always sneaking inside and making a mess. Besides, Da—uh, Mr. Van Haver and Kelli are allergic to cat hair."

"Is there anything they're not allergic to?" Miguel asked skeptically.

"Look, you don't understand. If Kelli's around cats, she breaks out in an ugly red rash," Leanna explained. "That would be a total disaster because—"

Miguel didn't give Leanna a chance to explain. "Yeah, it would be a real tragedy if Kelli got zits," he interrupted sarcastically. "What is she, some kind of princess? Her parents plaster the house with her pictures, and you get all upset because she might

99

break out. No wonder she's so stuck on herself."

"I like Kelli," Leanna said angrily. "How can you judge her? You don't even know her!"

"I don't want to know her!" Miguel burst out. "She's a selfish snob. She has nothing on her mind but fixing her hair, buying new clothes, and putting on makeup. Girls like that make me sick."

"Fine!" Leanna screamed. "If that's the way you feel, I guess you should leave! I don't need you criticizing my family!"

Miguel stepped back. He looked as stunned as if she had slapped him. "Why are you defending them? The Van Havers aren't your *family*. Don't let them come between us."

Leanna gripped the car door handle to keep her hands from shaking. She'd almost blown it a second ago! She'd have to be more careful.

"I meant my host family," Leanna said, her voice shaking. "I care about the Van Havers, Miguel. You don't understand—"

"You're right. I don't understand." Miguel's voice was quiet, but icy cold. "I don't understand why you let them push you around. I thought you were the type of girl who'd stand up for herself." And with that, Miguel climbed in his car and drove off. He didn't kiss her good-bye or say, "I'll call you." He just backed out of the driveway and drove out of Leanna's life.

Leanna finished the lawn, then went upstairs and took a shower. Afterward, she wrapped a towel around her wet hair and slipped into her pink terry cloth robe. When she returned to her room, she found her mother sitting on her bed.

"Look, Mom," Leanna began before her mother could start lecturing. "I'm sorry I broke the rules. Just ground me for the rest of the month and get it over with, okay?"

"We'll stick with one week." Mrs. Van Haver crossed her legs and settled back against Leanna's pillow. "But we do need to talk."

"I'd rather be grounded," Leanna said.

Her mother was getting comfortable, as if she expected to be sitting there for a very long time.

"Dad and I don't enjoy punishing you," Mrs. Van Haver said. "But we worry when you do something dangerous, like go out alone at night with a boy we don't know. Then, today, when we came back to get my credit card and saw a strange car in the driveway, we almost called the police. That wreck looked like something a homeless person would live in."

"Mom!" Leanna cried. She sat down on the bed next to her mother and covered her face with her hands. She'd thought her day had been as humiliating as it could possibly be, but it had just gotten worse. Her mother had almost had Miguel arrested!

"What was I supposed to think?" her mother demanded. "You weren't allowed to have friends over."

"I said I was sorry!" Leanna cried.

Mrs. Van Haver laid her hand gently on Leanna's shoulder. "Honey, why do you feel you have to sneak around with Miguel? Dad and I would never stop you from dating whomever you like. Is there a reason why you didn't tell us about Miguel? Are you ashamed of him?"

Leanna's head snapped up. "No! Miguel's a great guy!"

"He's Filipino, isn't he?"

"So what?" Leanna demanded. "That's nothing to be ashamed of." She pushed back her bathrobe sleeve and held her brown arm next to her mother's pale one. "*I'm* a Filipina, Mom. Or haven't you noticed?"

Leanna's mother ignored her remark. "Your father called while you were in the shower," she said, still in a calm, gentle voice. "He seems to think I don't want you visiting him. He accused me of standing in the way of your Philippine heritage. Do you know where he got such a wrong idea, Leanna?"

"Uh, no," Leanna mumbled. She ducked her head, rubbing the towel vigorously over her wet hair.

"Leanna, look at me when I'm talking to you."

Leanna searched her mother's face, looking for a connection between them. She saw nothing of herself in her mother's round blue-gray eyes, pale skin, and long blond hair. Alison Van Haver could have been Kelli's mother easier than Leanna's.

"I hope I've never said anything to give you a bad impression of your father, or of being a Filipina," Mrs. Van Haver said, twisting her hands together. "I want you to be proud of your background."

"I am, Mom." Leanna pulled the towel off her head and raked her fingers though her long, wet hair.

Mrs. Van Haver got a comb from the dresser and handed it to her daughter. "Can we meet Miguel next week?"

"I don't think so." Remembering the bad things Miguel had said about the Van Havers, Leanna doubted she'd ever see him again. She swallowed a sob in her throat. "Miguel has a traditional Filipino family. He speaks Tagalog and everything. I'm afraid I'm too—too American for him."

"You could learn about the Philippines," her mother suggested. "Talk to your father. Didn't he give you some books and cassettes?"

"Yeah." Leanna pulled a comb through her hair. "But what if it doesn't work? Miguel wants an old-fashioned Filipina. I'm afraid I'll never measure up."

Mrs. Van Haver frowned. "Leanna, you shouldn't learn about the Philippines to please Miguel, or even your father. This is something you should do for yourself. Only you can decide how far you should go and what you're comfortable with. Don't change how you are to fit some guy's idea of the perfect girl. Let Miguel see the *real* you, and then let him decide if you're worth knowing."

Leanna remembered what Miguel had said about Kelli. "But what if he decided I'm . . . selfish and snobby?"

"Then *he* isn't worth knowing." Mrs. Van Haver leaned over to hug her daughter. "I know this is hard for you to believe right now, but there'll be other guys in your life. And speaking of other guys, honey . . . have you thought about Scott?"

Not lately, Leanna felt like saying. It was odd, but when Miguel was around, she completely forgot Scott even existed.

"Well . . . I'm still trying to figure out what to do about him," Leanna admitted.

"I'm sure you'll make the right decision," Mrs. Van Haver said, getting up from Leanna's bed. "Just one more question. Who put Kelli's modeling portfolio pictures in all the frames in the hall?"

They must have been the only eight-by-tens Kelli could find, Leanna thought. No wonder Miguel thought Kelli was stuck on herself!

"It was my idea," Leanna confessed. "I'll put the family pictures back."

Hugging a pillow to her chest, Leanna watched her mother walk out of the room. She could tell from her mother's brisk pace that Mrs. Van Haver thought her daughter's problems were solved. Which only showed Leanna how truly clueless her mother actually was.

Let Miguel see the real you. Yeah, right. Miguel had made it pretty clear that he didn't want the *real* Leanna. Or at least, not her American half.

Leanna rolled off the bed and peered under it. She thrust her arm into the dusty darkness and pulled out everything she touched. A pink sock, a blue bedroom slipper, the pen she'd lost . . . and a sealed cassette tape of *Conversational Tagalog.*

Leanna tore off the cellophane and popped the tape in her stereo.

"How are you?" a man's voice asked. *"Kumustá ka?"*

"Kumustá ka?" Leanna repeated. *Miguel might not come back,* she thought, *but if he does, I'll be ready for him!*

Chapter Eleven

"WHERE ARE YOU going? *Saan ka pupunta?*" the narrator on the Tagalog tape asked.

That was an easy one. "*Saan ka pupunta,*" Leanna repeated. She'd stayed up late Saturday night, playing the tapes and studying the books Carlos had given her. Now it was Sunday afternoon, and she was practicing her Tagalog phrases again.

"I am going shopping," said the tape. "*Magshashaping.*"

"I could be *shaping* at the mall right this minute, if I wasn't grounded." Kelli and two of her friends had gone *shaping* this afternoon.

"Could I come with you? *Pwede ba akong sumama sa iyo?*"

"*Pwede—pwede—*you've got to be kidding!" Leanna exclaimed. Some Tagalog expressions were so easy, but others used way too many letters. She reached over and stopped the tape. "Who invented this language, anyway?"

There was a tap on her bedroom door. "Leanna, may I come in?" her stepfather's voice called.

"*Tuloy ka!*" Leanna shouted. Now that was a good Tagalog expression: easy to pronounce, easy to remember, and much nicer sounding than the English words "come in."

"What?" Dad asked.

Leanna opened the door. "I used Tagalog to say come in."

Mr. Van Haver walked into Leanna's room. "Honey, you have—what's this?" he asked, looking at the poster of a Filipina in ballet slippers and a white tutu hanging over Leanna's bed. Yesterday a poster of Brad Pitt had been hanging there.

"That's Lisa Macuja. She was a famous dancer with the Russian ballet." Leanna opened her closet door. A poster of another young Filipina was taped to the inside. "And this is Lea Salonga. Did you know she was the singing voice of Princess Jasmine in the Disney movie *Aladdin*?"

"No, I didn't," Mr. Van Haver admitted, smiling. "Where did you get these posters?"

"Carlos sent them to me a long time ago. He thought they would inspire me or something," Leanna explained. "I'm trying to learn Tagalog, and I figured these would put me in the mood." She glanced anxiously at her stepfather's face.

"That's a great idea. A second language is a real advantage in today's world."

"But I'm not sure how useful these tapes are," Leanna complained. "They have all kinds of touristy expressions, like 'Where is the hotel?' and 'Where is the airport?' But there aren't many everyday words."

"I could check the language section at the library," Dad offered. "I'll bring home whatever I find on the Philippines." Mr. Van Haver worked at the large branch library in downtown Sacramento.

"You don't have to." Leanna closed her closet door.

"No, I want to. I've been thinking that maybe the whole family should go to the Philippines for a vacation," Mr. Van Haver said. "Would you like that?"

"Cool," Leanna said faintly. She could hardly believe it. She'd been afraid he'd feel hurt or threatened if she showed too much interest in the Philippines, but instead, he was going out of his way to help.

"Oh, I almost forgot what I came in here for," Dad said, pausing in the doorway. "Scott's downstairs. I told him you were grounded, but he said it was important. You may see him for a few minutes. He's in the family room."

Facing Scott was the last thing Leanna wanted to do right now. Last night, she'd made up her mind that the only fair thing to do was to stop going out with Scott. Still, she wasn't looking forward to breaking his heart.

And here he was. Leanna stood in the doorway of the family room, watching Scott gaze at the Van

Havers' videotapes. As usual, Scott was wearing one of his vintage outfits, faded jeans and a flowered Hawaiian shirt. Also as usual, he didn't notice Leanna was there until she cleared her throat.

"Oh, hi," Scott said, turning away from the video shelves. "Um, your dad said you're grounded, so I'll only stay a minute."

Scott sat awkwardly on the edge of the sofa. Leanna sat down next to him, but she couldn't bring herself to meet his eyes. *I know why I'm so nervous,* she thought, *but what's Scott so jumpy about?*

Scott cleared his throat. "Listen, about Friday night. Glenn was totally obnoxious, and I'm sorry—"

"It's okay," Leanna interrupted.

Scott shook his head. "No, it's not okay. Double-dating with Glenn and Kelli wasn't my idea of a fun night out, but since *you* wanted to go, you should have tried to get along with him. The whole night was a disaster, and you just made it worse."

Leanna stared at Scott. "You want *me* to apologize to *you?*" she asked indignantly. She couldn't believe what she was hearing. Her sympathy for Scott quickly evaporated. "You've got to be kidding."

"Listen, Leanna . . . ," Scott began, drumming his fingers on the coffee table. "I really came here because I think we need to talk about us."

Leanna took a deep breath. "Things haven't been going so well lately, have they?"

"I really like you." Scott reached out and took her hand. "But ever since you got back from San Diego, I feel like we're miles apart. Like there's

110

something in the way. Are you . . . are you seeing someone else?"

"Not really," Leanna said. And it was the truth. After yesterday's disaster, she didn't think she'd ever see Miguel again. She squeezed Scott's hand and then pulled away. "But that's not important. What matters is that I think we're moving in different directions. Maybe we're still dating because we're comfortable with each other. It's just not exciting anymore."

"I know what you mean. So . . . does this mean we're breaking up?" Scott asked softly.

Leanna swallowed hard. "Is—is that what you want?"

"I want to be friends," Scott said. "But I agree with you. Things just aren't right with us anymore."

Leanna felt her eyes fill with tears. *This is totally stupid!* she thought. *I want to break up with Scott. So why am I getting weepy?*

As she wiped impatiently at her eyes, a horrible thought occurred to her. Maybe she wanted to break up with Scott, but she didn't want *Scott* to break up with *her*! She didn't mind dumping a guy, but she couldn't stand to be dumped herself. She was nothing but an egotist! She was as bad as . . . as Glenn Garrick!

Scott left a few minutes later, and Leanna ran upstairs, throwing herself facedown on her bed. She didn't want to cry, but somehow she couldn't help herself.

111

But I don't love Scott, Leanna thought. She sat up and dried her eyes. Scott had been right: He and Leanna had grown apart. She and Scott simply weren't meant to be together.

"Miguel!" Leanna gasped when she answered the phone later that afternoon. Her heart gave a crazy jump as she sank into a kitchen chair.

"I'm at work, so I can't talk long," Miguel said. Leanna heard him take a deep breath. "I, uh, want to apologize for yesterday. What your host family does is none of my business. I was totally out of line."

"Apology accepted," Leanna said.

"Cool," Miguel said. There was a long silence.

"Miguel? Are you still there?"

"Yeah. I—I was just wondering . . . would you like to go out with me? On a real date?" Miguel asked.

"I'm grounded," Leanna reminded him. She couldn't help smiling. Just a few hours ago, her life had been a disaster, and now everything was beginning to look up.

"I mean next Saturday," Miguel said. "My cousin Rosalia is having a party for her eighteenth birthday. She lives in San Francisco. Want to drive down with me?"

"Sure. That sounds fun," Leanna said, a twinge of disappointment in her voice.

Miguel sounded as if he thought his cousin's birthday party was a major deal. Of course, Leanna would be happy to see him under any circumstances; but couldn't he have thought of something more private . . . more romantic for their first real date?

"Great!" Miguel said. There was no mistaking his happiness.

Leanna felt warm clear down to her toes.

"I'll pick you up at four," Miguel said. "I know you'll like Rosalia, and you'll love the party. If you're homesick for a real Philippine celebration, this is it."

Leanna hung up, feeling both elated and puzzled. She had a date with Miguel! But why had he called his cousin's party a "Philippine celebration"? As far as she knew, Filipinos didn't celebrate their birthdays any differently than Americans. Carlos had sent her normal birthday cards and gifts each year.

Maybe Miguel meant they'd serve Philippine food at the party, or that all the guests would be Filipino.

Just in case, she'd call Carlos and ask him if there was anything special she should know about Philippine birthday parties. *This is my big chance,* Leanna thought. *I can't blow it now!*

Chapter Twelve

"NO, THERE'S NOTHING different about Philippine birthdays," Carlos said. It was Monday after school. "We have parties, just like Americans."

"Thanks, Carlos. I'm going to a birthday party with a—a Filipino friend on Saturday," Leanna said. "And I want to do everything right."

"I'm glad you're meeting other Filipinos, learning about your heritage," Carlos said. "Hey, did I ever tell you about the Bontoc tribe? The women are known for their weaving. Some of the tribes even believe that their weaving is magical, and all powers will be lost if a section of weaving is cut."

"Cool," Leanna said. Sure, Carlos was lecturing her again, but somehow it didn't seem as boring as usual. Leanna wanted to know all about the Philippines now.

"I could send you a Bontoc blanket," Carlos offered. "My great-aunt made it years ago. It's lemon yellow and royal blue. It's very striking."

"Thanks," Leanna said. "I'd love to have it." She could hardly believe her father was giving her such a precious family heirloom. He could have saved it for one of the boys . . . but he'd offered it to her.

"I can mail it tomorrow," Carlos said softly. "But I'd rather give you the blanket in person. Have you decided when you'd like to visit?"

"Next month, I guess," Leanna said uncertainly. She couldn't go to San Diego now, and leave Miguel. "I'll call you when I know for sure," Leanna added. She hung up, feeling bad. Her conversation with Carlos had been going so well. Why did he have to ruin it by pressuring her to see him?

"That's Miguel!" Leanna cried when the doorbell rang the next Saturday afternoon. She sprang up from the kitchen table, where she'd been sitting with her parents and Kelli. "You guys stay right here. Don't go anywhere!"

"We've been waiting here for the last ten minutes," Mrs. Van Haver said, smiling as she closed her magazine. "We promise to stay put."

"We're looking forward to meeting Miguel," Mr. Van Haver added, closing a book on the Philippines he'd been reading.

Leanna hurried down the hallway, grabbing framed photographs on her way. Since her parents were home, she hadn't been able to replace them

116

with anything else, or even remove them earlier. The best she could do was get rid of the telltale family pictures at the last minute.

Yanking open the hall closet, Leanna tossed an armload of framed photos on the floor. Then she zipped along the other wall, pulled down the rest of the pictures, and threw them in the closet, too. Shutting the door, Leanna quickly adjusted her pink cotton sweater, combed her fingers through her hair, and reached out to open the front door.

"Hi, Miguel," Leanna said, hoping he wouldn't notice that she was practically gasping for breath after her sprint down the hall. "Come on in."

Leanna couldn't help but stare at Miguel as he stepped into the hallway. His black hair, usually worn in straight bangs, was slicked back. He wore polished black shoes, a white dress shirt, and a pearl gray tuxedo with a black bow tie and cummerbund. He looked totally hot. But why was he wearing a tux to his cousin's birthday party?

"You're not ready." Miguel frowned at Leanna's black jeans and pink sweater.

"That's because—you're early!" Leanna said, fumbling for words. "You said you were coming at four-thirty."

"I'm sure I said four." Miguel's eyebrows drew together, and he shifted from foot to foot, looking uncomfortable.

"Oh—then I guess I misunderstood. My fault." Leanna tried to laugh. It came out a nervous cackle. "No problem, I'll be ready in five minutes."

117

Yeah, right!

"Can I meet your host parents?" Miguel asked.

"Sure. This way." Leanna led Miguel down the hall to the kitchen. She wasn't sure if she wanted to kiss him or strangle him. Why hadn't he told her the party was formal? He'd acted as if she should have *known,* which didn't make sense unless all Philippine birthday parties were formal affairs. And if they were, why hadn't Carlos told her?

Leanna's family looked up when she brought Miguel into the kitchen. Her parents and Kelli looked as startled as Leanna had when they saw what Miguel was wearing. Fortunately, they were too polite to say anything.

"This is Miguel Sarmiento," Leanna said. "Miguel, you've already met Kelli." Leanna glanced sharply at Kelli, hoping her stepsister would remember her cue.

"Uh—hi, Miguel," Kelli gulped. "These are my parents, Mr. and Mrs. Van Haver."

"How are you?" Miguel asked, shaking hands first with Mrs. Van Haver, then her husband. He didn't seem to think it was odd that Kelli had performed the introductions, and Leanna sighed with relief.

"Nice tux, son," Mr. Van Haver said as he clasped Miguel's hand. He glanced at Leanna's sweater and jeans with a puzzled expression.

"Well, I'd better go upstairs and change," Leanna said. "Can you come help me, Kelli?"

Kelli jumped up from the table. "Yeah, sure."

"Sit down, Miguel," Mrs. Van Haver offered. "Let's get better acquainted."

Leanna groaned. That was just what she was afraid of: her parents asking Miguel questions, or vice versa. What if Miguel asked about being a "host family," or Mrs. Van Haver called Leanna "my daughter"? Still, Leanna didn't have any other choice. She'd just get dressed as quickly as possible and hope nothing awful happened while she was gone.

When they were safely out of the kitchen, Leanna felt Kelli grab her arm. "What's with Miguel's outfit?" Kelli scoffed. "Your boyfriends have the weirdest fashion sense. First Scott with his thrift-shop stuff, and now Miguel in a tux! Why's he so dressed up?"

"Don't ask me." Leanna hurried up the steps two at a time. "He said we were going to a birthday party. I thought he meant at the girl's house."

"If so, she must live in a palace," Kelli said, following Leanna upstairs. "What are you going to wear?"

"I wish I could wear something of yours. All I have is this long dress." Leanna burst into her bedroom and pulled open the closet.

Quickly, Leanna pulled off her jeans and sweater and stepped into the full-skirted gown. The underskirt was stiff pink taffeta, and the bodice and overskirt were made of white lace.

"I look like a bridesmaid," Leanna complained. It was hard to walk in the enormous skirt. She'd bought this gown for the Miss Cocoa-Tropic Tan

119

Pageant—that was before she'd agreed to spend the summer with Carlos's family. Wearing it onstage, she would have felt like a princess. In her small bedroom, with her hair hanging loose, she just felt silly.

"Sit down," Kelli said. "I'll fix your hair while you do your makeup."

Leanna sat in front of her mirror. "Why didn't Miguel tell me to dress up for this party? Either he's really dense, or he's trying to embarrass me on purpose."

"I vote for both," Kelli said. She piled Leanna's hair on top of her head and began fastening it with pins.

"Personally, I'm through with guys. Can you believe Glenn Garrick asked me out again? Well, I told him no way. Until somebody decent comes along, I'm hanging out with my girlfriends."

"Good for you," Leanna said. She reached for a makeup brush. "I know there are lots of losers out there . . . and I hope Miguel's not one of them."

"The party is from six to nine, so I'll have Leanna home by eleven," Miguel told the Van Havers. "We're having dinner at the Regency Hotel, then there's a live band for dancing."

"It sounds wonderful," Mrs. Van Haver said. She refilled Miguel's iced-tea glass. "When Leanna said she was going to a birthday party, I imagined a bunch of teens eating cake and listening to CDs in your cousin's basement."

"But didn't Leanna tell you this is Rosalia's

eighteenth birthday?" Miguel asked. He took a sip of tea.

The Van Havers exchanged glances. Mrs. Van Haver shrugged. "Is there something different about an eighteenth birthday?"

"Not for a guy," Miguel explained. Obviously, the Van Havers knew nothing about Philippine culture, but he didn't mind telling them. They seemed really interested, especially Mr. Van Haver. Miguel had noticed that he had been reading a book called *The Philippine Chronicles.*

"When a girl turns eighteen, her father throws a formal party at the best hotel in town," Miguel went on. "Originally, the idea was to present her to the single men of the community, and she was expected to marry within a year. I don't know many Filipinas who'd go along with that now, especially my cousin. But their debuts are always a blast, anyway. I guess they don't want to miss out on a huge party and tons of gifts."

"And you say this is an important Philippine tradition?" Mr. Van Haver asked. He selected a piece of hard candy from a bowl on the table.

"Of course. *Every* Filipina, even a girl from a totally Americanized family, looks forward to making her debut. My sister, Carolina, is fifteen," Miguel told them. "She couldn't be more Americanized if she had blond hair and freckles, and even she's already talking about where she'll make her debut."

"Do you think Leanna would like a debut party?" Mrs. Van Haver asked, sounding worried.

"I'd like her to have one, if it's part of her heritage. But I'm not sure if we'd do everything right."

"Oh, don't worry about that," Miguel reassured the Van Havers. "Leanna's father will make all the arrangements. By that time she'll be living with him, right?"

"Excuse me?" Mrs. Van Haver asked. Miguel couldn't understand why her face had suddenly turned a chalky white.

Mr. Van Haver put an arm around his wife's shoulder. "Has Leanna talked about moving in with her father?" he asked Miguel.

Miguel couldn't understand what was going on. One minute, the Van Havers seemed normal and friendly; the next, they were huddled together, and Mrs. Van Haver looked as if she were about to cry.

Before Miguel could answer, Leanna glided into the kitchen with Kelli right behind her. Leanna's dress floated around her like a pink cloud. Her hair was piled on top of her head and fastened with rhinestone combs. She looked absolutely beautiful.

Miguel got up from his chair. Leanna looked so much like a princess, he almost bowed. "Nice dress," he said. "But don't you know you're not supposed to look prettier than the debutante herself?"

"Debutante?" Leanna repeated, wrinkling her forehead.

"My cousin Rosalia." Miguel wasn't surprised that Leanna had forgotten his cousin's name. With all his brothers and sisters, and now his cousin, there were so many names to remember.

122

"Leanna, Miguel, wait right there. I'll get my camera." Mr. Van Haver patted his wife's shoulder as if reassuring her. Miguel still had no idea why Mrs. Van Haver was upset.

As he posed for a bunch of pictures with Leanna, Miguel thought about the Van Havers. They were an odd family, all right. They seemed attached to Leanna, but almost *too* attached. As if they didn't want to let her go back to her real family, the Maligs.

As Leanna said good-bye to the Van Havers, Miguel resolved to put the overprotective host family out of his mind. He didn't want them to ruin the magical night ahead of them.

Chapter Thirteen

"I STILL CAN'T believe they valet parked your car," Leanna said as she and Miguel walked into the plush lobby of the Regency Hotel in San Francisco. It was by far the most luxurious place she'd ever visited. All the elevators were made of glass, and sparkling jewels that looked like diamonds hung from the chandeliers. Leanna no longer felt uncomfortable in her pageant gown. She only wished she had long white gloves and a tiara to go with it.

Miguel laughed. "My car was probably a major letdown after all those BMWs in front of us."

Leanna laughed, too. The look on the valet's face had been priceless. For a few seconds, she'd been sure the man was going to tell Miguel to park the battered old car himself.

"Hey, there's my sister Carrie," Miguel said,

pointing at a pretty dark-haired girl. "Come on, I'll introduce you. Maybe she knows which room the party's in."

They walked over to a slender girl standing between two gilded doors. She wore a long black silk dress, and her hair was very short, except in front where it stuck out in spikes.

This was Miguel's sister? Leanna was surprised that someone in Miguel's ultraconservative family would have such a daring haircut.

"Hey, Carrie," Miguel said. "This is Leanna Malig."

"Nice to meet you, Leanna." Carrie reached out to shake hands. Her nails were painted a deep purple that was almost black. "I'd introduce you to *my* date, but he's in the rest room."

At that moment, one of the gold doors opened and a totally hot guy strolled out. *Strolled* was the right word, Leanna thought; his graceful, rolling walk was as familiar to Leanna as his shoulder-length hair and single silver earring. She saw them every day at school.

What's Eddie Alvarez doing here? Eddie wasn't part of Leanna's crowd at Bayside Academy, but she knew who he was. Quickly, Leanna turned her back, hoping Eddie would walk by without recognizing her.

"Eddie!" Carrie called. "Come here and meet my brother and his date."

Leanna wanted to sink right through the floor. Carrie was here with *Eddie*? Eddie had been in fashion shows with Leanna. He knew her name. Maybe she should run into the ladies' room and stay there until Carrie and Eddie left. But it was too late. Eddie was standing beside Carrie, and from the way he was smiling at Leanna, she knew she was doomed.

"Eddie Alvarez, this is my brother Miguel," Carrie said. The guys shook hands. "And this is—"

"I already know you," Eddie said. "You go to Bayside, right? Your name is Leanna—Leanna—"

Leanna felt weak. *Don't say it*, she prayed. *Don't say Leanna Van Haver!*

Eddie smiled apologetically. "Sorry, I can't remember your last name."

"Leanna Malig," Leanna almost whispered. Close one!

But Leanna wasn't out of danger yet. Now Carrie was staring at her with a fascinated expression.

"You go to Bayside?" Carrie asked. "What are you, an actress? A singer? Have you ever been on TV?"

"Why would Leanna be on TV?" Miguel broke in. He glanced from Leanna to Carrie with a puzzled expression.

"I'm starving!" Leanna exclaimed, trying to change the subject. "Let's find the party. Aren't they serving dinner at six?"

"Yeah. I think it's this way." Miguel started down a long carpeted hall, but he still looked confused. Leaning closer to Leanna, he asked, "What's this about you being on TV?"

"Not me." Leanna laughed nervously. "Some of

127

the kids who go to Bayside want to be actors, but I'm not into that."

"No, Leanna's in the modeling division, with me," Eddie interrupted. He and Carrie had followed Miguel and Leanna down the hall. "Bayside's like college, you know? You can take classes in different things—filmmaking, acting, dance—but you pick one area to focus on, sort of like your major. I picked modeling because I'm not very good at memorizing lines."

"Modeling and dancing. That's pretty cool," Miguel said in a pleasant voice. "I don't know why I thought Bayside was such a tough academic school." Miguel's eyes were cold as they focused on Leanna.

"I said Bayside was hard to get into—and it is!" Leanna snapped, her eyes glaring. "You have to have top grades *and* talent! Our performing arts classes are in *addition* to regular subjects like algebra and science. Our school day is twice as long, and we work twice as hard."

Miguel looked stunned.

"That's totally cool, Leanna!" Carrie cheered. "My brother thinks anthropology is the only respectable career in the world."

Carrie continued talking, telling Leanna that she wanted to own a clothing store. But Leanna only half-listened. She kept watching Miguel as he walked slowly, staring straight ahead.

Outside the party, an older man in a dark suit took their invitations, then checked a long list. "Table twenty," he said, waving them through the doors.

Miguel held the door open for Leanna, and they stepped into a grand ballroom. Half the floor was polished wood. At the far end, on a raised platform, an orchestra played soft, soothing music. Leanna had never been to a birthday party like this before. Once, Glenn Garrick had tried to impress everyone by hiring a band for his party, but that had turned out to be four guys with guitars and a keyboard. This orchestra had violins, a piano, and a cello!

The other side of the room, carpeted in plush royal blue, held dozens of round tables set with white linen cloths, crystal goblets, and gleaming silver. Seated at the tables, talking and laughing as waiters refilled their water glasses, were people of all ages. Nearly all of them were Filipino.

Everything is so beautiful. But I don't belong here. I'm an imposter. . . .

"No, Eddie," Carrie giggled, breaking Leanna out of her worried thoughts. "We have to go through the receiving line first."

Eddie got up from his seat. "You'll have to excuse me," he said. "I don't know anything about eighteenth birthday traditions."

"It's a lot like what you told me about fifteenth birthdays in Mexico," Carrie said, taking Eddie's arm. She glanced over at Leanna. "Did you know, if we were Mexican, we wouldn't have to wait till we were eighteen to get a bash like this? Oh, well, I'm an American now, so maybe I can talk my parents into a sweet *sixteen* party instead of a debut like this."

Miguel offered Leanna his arm, ignoring his

sister's voice. "C'mon, Leanna. Let's say hello to the birthday girl."

Leanna stood between Miguel and Carrie as they approached several elegantly dressed people standing in a line. Guests were walking by and shaking hands with them. *This is just like a wedding,* Leanna thought. She wished Miguel would tell her what to do; but of course he assumed she knew already.

"Just shake hands with Rosalia, her brother, and her parents," Leanna heard Carrie tell Eddie. "But when you shake hands with her grandparents and great-grandmother, do *this.*" Carrie grasped Eddie's right hand and touched it to her forehead. "Putting an elder's right hand to your head shows respect."

Eddie shook hands with Rosalia. She wore a long white gown and gloves that reached past her elbows. Then Leanna watched him clasp the hand of a tiny gray-haired woman and gently touch it to his forehead. The small woman's face broke into a radiant smile.

Leanna felt silly. But if Eddie could do it, so could she. She shook hands with the younger members of Rosalia's family, then touched the old woman's hand to her head. She was rewarded by a warm smile. The old woman said something to Miguel in Tagalog that seemed to make him blush.

"What did she say?" Leanna asked as they sat back at their table.

"It was nothing." Miguel took a quick sip of his water and blushed even deeper.

"I heard what she said." Carrie unfolded her cloth napkin in her lap and smiled teasingly at her brother. "Great-grandmother said you were a nice girl and that Miguel should marry you."

"What's this about my little cousin getting married?" a teasing female voice asked. "No way! Not unless I'm married first!"

A Filipina with straight, shoulder-length dark hair slipped into the empty seat next to Miguel. She was wearing a gorgeous gown of ice blue lace.

"This is my cousin Christina. She's a sophomore at the University of California at Berkeley," Miguel added. "She's a history major."

"This is Leanna Malig and Eddie Alvarez," Miguel told Christina. "They're *models.*"

"Cool! I've never met a model before. What's it like being in front of a camera all the time?"

Miguel's jaw dropped, and Leanna couldn't help giggling. She knew he'd expected his college-age cousin to think modeling was as frivolous as he did.

After Leanna finished telling Christina how much fun it was to be a model, everyone began to eat. They were served a cold shrimp appetizer, then a fresh green salad. But Miguel didn't touch a bite of either.

"Next course is the *lechón,*" Carrie announced. She nudged Miguel in the ribs. "I think Eddie should take the first serving, don't you, Miguel?"

Lechón was always served at Philippine celebrations. Dora had made it on Leanna's first night in San Diego. Leanna smiled, remembering how confused she'd been when Dora had invited her to take the first serving.

"I don't know if I'm ready for this," Eddie said warily. He looked around the table. Everyone was smiling or laughing. "What is *lechón,* anyway?"

Carrie began, "It's—"

"I think Leanna should explain about *lechón.*" Miguel's voice rose, drowning his sister out.

Leanna was more angry than afraid. She knew Miguel was trying to trap her. He must have figured out somehow that she was an imposter. Well, Miguel Sarmiento was in for a major surprise.

Leanna smiled sweetly as she began to explain. "*Lechón* is a whole roast pig, and it's served at every Philippine feast. At a big party like this, there'll probably be a *lechón* for each table. It's tradition to ask the *dayo*—or foreigner—to take the first piece. It's a great honor."

"Cool. I love roast pork," Eddie said, sounding relieved.

Leanna stared steadily at Miguel. He met her eyes for a moment, then dropped his gaze. Leanna felt elated. She knew not to tell Eddie *how* to take the first serving. That was the whole joke, why everyone laughed at offering him the first serving.

Two servers approached their table. One carried a folding table, the other a large platter with a silver cover. They set up a platter on the folding table, then removed the cover. A whole roast pig with crisp brown skin grinned at them with a bright red apple stuck in it's mouth.

"Go ahead, Eddie," Carrie urged. "Take the first piece."

Eddie picked up his knife and fork and stood up from the table.

"No, no," Leanna said, with a sideways glance at Miguel. "You're not allowed to use utensils."

Miguel looked surprised. Leanna smiled smugly. She'd proven to Miguel that she knew what she was doing. She wasn't the *dayo* at this feast!

Eddie raised his eyebrows. "How am I supposed to get a piece with my bare hands?"

"Figure it out," Christina said, laughing.

Eddie circled the pig, eyeing the smooth brown skin. "What do I do?" he asked. "C'mon, Carrie. Help me out."

Leanna decided to help. "It's easy," she said. "If you pull off all the skin, the server will carve the meat."

"Thanks." Eddie tugged on the skin near the pig's shoulder. Nothing happened.

"This stuff is stuck on tight!" Eddie exclaimed. Miguel's cousins dissolved in laughter.

"Pull off the ear," Miguel said, smiling a devilish grin. A brave Eddie grabbed the ear and successfully pulled the skin off. Everyone applauded as Eddie triumphantly sat down and the servers took over.

Leanna didn't know Eddie very well, but she was liking him more and more as the evening went on. Every time something strange happened, Carrie

133

had carefully explained it to Eddie. And Leanna had listened intently, luckily avoiding any embarrassing mistakes.

After dinner, the dancing began. As the orchestra switched to a slow, dreamy number, Miguel held out his hand to Leanna. She followed him onto the dance floor and draped her arms around his neck. Leanna closed her eyes, swaying to the soft, romantic music.

"So, you're a model," Miguel whispered close to her ear.

Leanna's eyes flew open. "Do you have a problem with that?" she asked defensively, pulling away from him.

"Leanna, listen." Miguel's voice was so soft and gentle, she relaxed back into his arms. "I don't care if you want to be a model. I just want you to be happy. I was upset before because I thought you'd lied to me about your private school. Then I began wondering what else you'd lied about."

"I never lied about Bayside," Leanna pointed out. "I said it was an exclusive private school, and it is. I never said it *wasn't* a performing arts school."

"I know," Miguel said, pulling her closer. "It's just that I—I was hurt by a girl before . . . lied to. It's hard for me to learn to trust again." Miguel took a deep breath. "Forgive me?"

"Yeah," Leanna whispered, the butterflies fluttering in her belly again. *But will you forgive me when you learn the truth?* she wondered.

"I'd never lie to you," Miguel promised against her hair.

Leanna's heart sank. This was *not* a good time to tell him the truth about the Van Havers. If Miguel freaked out when he'd just *thought* she'd lied, what would he do when he found out she really *had*?

Chapter Fourteen

"OH, IT WAS a girl's *eighteenth* birthday party," Carlos apologized on the phone the next morning. "I didn't know you were going to a debutante ball. I wish you would have told me. I could have explained it all to you."

"So all Filipinos do this?" Leanna asked, shifting the phone to her other ear. She reached into an upper cabinet for a box of cornflakes. "Why didn't you mention it before?"

"I didn't think you'd be interested," Carlos replied. "You never cared about any Philippine customs before."

"Well . . . uh, this is different," Leanna said. She poured some cereal into a bowl. "What teenage girl *wouldn't* jump at the chance to dress like a princess and have a major bash? I may be modern, but I'm not *stupid*."

Her father's hearty laugh rolled out of the receiver. "I guess I don't know much about teenage girls," he admitted. "I'm more familiar with little boys. But now that we're settled in our new house, I hope that will change." Carlos's voice became more serious. "Feel free to visit anytime, Leanna. It's only a two-hour flight. You don't even have to stay overnight if you don't want to."

While her father was speaking, Leanna thought about his offer. Meeting Miguel's relatives last night and seeing how close they were made Leanna realize how much she missed Carlos and the boys. Visiting the Maligs would also be a good opportunity to practice her Tagalog and to learn things about the Philippines that didn't appear in books.

"Well, I'm busy the next two weekends," Leanna said, checking the wall calendar by the phone. "And then it's Halloween."

"Oh, the boys would love to spend Halloween with you. We don't celebrate it in the Philippines, so this will be their first time trick-or-treating. They could really use an expert to show them how it's done."

Leanna was tempted. It would be fun to see her little half brothers all dressed up. "What are they wearing?" she asked.

"I'm not exactly sure. Dora wants them to be pirates or ghosts, but the boys have their hearts set on being—what did they call it? Teenage Troll Troopers. Juan wants to be Jimmy the Blue Trooper, and Tomas wants to be Kirby the Purple Trooper."

"*Teenage Troll Troopers* is a cartoon show. All the little kids watch it," Leanna explained.

"Well, we'll have an American Halloween, and the next day we'll celebrate the Feast of All Saints," Carlos explained. "It's one of the most important holidays in the Philippines."

Leanna flipped the calendar to November. November first, the day after Halloween, was a Monday! If she accepted Carlos's invitation, she could attend a Philippine celebration *and* skip school!

Of course, she'd miss her friend Sara's Halloween party. She'd been planning to introduce Miguel to all her friends there.

But I'm a Filipina, Leanna reminded herself. *And family is more important than friends.*

"I'd love to come," Leanna heard herself say. Once the words were out, Leanna was surprised that she really meant them.

The next day, Leanna wore her *terno* to school and tucked a red silk flower into her loose hair. She'd brought her Tagalog phrase book to study during lunch and she hoped that dressing the part would help her learn faster.

As Leanna set her tray down next to Kelli's, the other girls at the lunch table looked up and smiled. Wendy, DeShaun, and Sara had been friends with Kelli and Leanna since freshman year.

"So, how was your big date with Miguel?" DeShaun asked, crunching into a carrot stick.

"It was awesome!" Leanna unwrapped a straw and stuck it into her milk carton. "The hotel was like a palace, and the music was great."

"Who was the band?" Sara asked. Since shaving her head, Sara was into seventies punk and heavy metal.

"It was an orchestra, silly," Leanna replied. "And dancing with Miguel was the best part. It was so romantic!"

Wendy twirled some spaghetti around a plastic fork. "You really like this guy, don't you? So . . . when do we get to meet Mr. Perfect?"

Before Leanna could answer, Kelli set down her soda can with a loud bang. "I've met Miguel, and he's far from perfect. Didn't you say he lived in a grass shack in the Philippines and hunted water buffalo?"

"He *hunts* buffalo?" DeShaun asked accusingly. She was a vegetarian and very concerned about animal rights. "Maybe you'd better think twice about this guy, Leanna."

"Miguel doesn't *hunt* buffalo!" Leanna shot a furious glance at her stepsister. What was Kelli's problem? "Miguel's family used to *own* a water buffalo. It was a pet."

"Excuse me," Kelli said in a phony-sweet voice. "I must have misunderstood."

Leanna's temper flared. She took a quick sip of milk to keep from shouting at Kelli. Leanna didn't want to argue with her in front of the entire cafeteria.

Sara glanced uneasily from Kelli to Leanna. "Uh, I guess we'll have to make up our own minds about whether Miguel is a major dude, or a major dud. You're bringing him to my Halloween party, right?"

Leanna nearly choked on her milk. "Actually, I need to talk to you about that," she said. "Sara, I—"

"Leanna doesn't celebrate American holidays like Halloween anymore," Kelli interrupted. "She got invited to a Philippine celebration that same weekend, so she's blowing you off, Sara."

Leanna was too shocked by Kelli's words to notice Sara's reaction. If Sara was hurt or angry, Leanna could apologize later. Right now, she had to find out what was up with Kelli.

"Can I talk to you in private?" Leanna asked through clenched teeth. Without giving Kelli a chance to reply, she grabbed Kelli's arm and practically dragged her out of the cafeteria.

"Why are you on my case?" Leanna demanded when she and Kelli were alone in a nearby rest room. "You're making Miguel sound like a major loser. You don't know anything about him or the Philippines!"

"And you do?" Kelli tossed back her long blond hair. "The way I see it, you were happy being American until your so-called father butted in. Then you ran off to San Diego, and when you got back, you had a Filipino boyfriend, and you think you're a Filipino yourself."

"Filipina, not Filipino." Leanna leaned against a sink. "Men are Filipino. Women are Filipina. And I am a Filipina . . . half."

"See what I mean? You think you're an expert on the Philippines." Kelli's face was red with what seemed like anger. "You don't care about anyone except the Maligs and Miguel. You're tossing aside everyone who cares about you. Scott, Sara, Mom, Dad . . . me—"

"Whoa, chill out a minute." Leanna suddenly understood why Kelli was upset. She reached across the sink and touched Kelli's hand. "I'm not leaving you," Leanna said softly. "I'm just going to visit the Maligs. You're totally overreacting."

"I'm not the only one," Kelli said in a shaky voice. "Mom's upset because you took down our family pictures both times Miguel came over. She thinks you're ashamed of us. And haven't you noticed how Dad's suddenly so interested in the Philippines? He thinks if he goes along with this—this sudden obsession of yours, you won't leave us!"

Kelli suddenly lunged at the paper towel dispenser and ripped out a handful of towels. She buried her face in them and leaned against the wall, sniffling loudly.

"C'mon, Kelli. You know you and Mom and Dad will always be part of my life. But I'm Filipina, too, and I can't ignore the Maligs anymore."

Leanna broke off as the rest room door opened. Wendy came in, darting a quick glance at Kelli,

142

who was still slumped against the wall. Wendy sidled over to Leanna.

"What's up?" Wendy whispered. "Why's Kelli crying?"

"I'm not crying," Kelli said in an icy tone. "My eyes are watering. I think my allergies are acting up." Kelli straightened her shoulders and pitched the wad of paper towels into the wastebasket. "I'm going to the nurse's office. I feel sick."

Leanna wished she could say or do something to make Kelli feel better. "We'll talk more at home," Leanna said as she moved aside to let Kelli pass.

Kelli paused in the doorway. "Just ask yourself this, Leanna. Does Miguel love *you,* or does he love the Filipino—excuse me, *Filipina*—you're pretending to be? Unless you intend to turn your back on your American family, you're going to have to tell him the truth about us. If he really loves you, he'll accept everything about you. He wouldn't want a relationship based on a lie."

As the door swung shut behind Kelli, Wendy patted Leanna's back. "Don't worry about Kelli. She's just jealous because she doesn't have a boyfriend right now, and you do."

Leanna nodded. "Could be," she said. But she knew that wasn't the problem. Leanna hated to admit it, but Kelli was right. By lying to Miguel, Leanna was rejecting her American family *and* her Philippine value of honesty. She'd have to find a way to tell Miguel the truth.

★　　★　　★

143

Leanna didn't see Miguel again until Saturday night. He was busy working at the theater, and though he called her a few times from work, he couldn't talk long.

I'll tell him in person, Leanna thought.

That night Miguel took her to Café Manila, where his parents worked. Leanna wore the yellow *terno* again, with her hair down and the red silk flower behind her ear.

"You look beautiful," Miguel said as he opened the car door for her. "Isn't that the dress you were wearing the day we met?"

Leanna slid into the front seat. "I didn't think you'd remember."

Miguel climbed into the car and fastened his seat belt. "Do you know what I thought the first time I saw you? I said to myself, I've got to meet that beautiful Filipina."

"That's nice," Leanna said faintly. She'd worn the *terno* because she knew Miguel had liked it. She'd hoped that if she looked her best, he'd be so dazzled he wouldn't freak out when she sprang the truth about her family.

"It must be so hard living with the Van Havers. You can't get more American than them. You must crave anything Philippine." Miguel took one hand off the steering wheel and gently held her hand. "I bet you miss your parents very much. When are you going home?"

"Halloween weekend," Leanna said. "That's part of what I wanted to talk to you about. The Maligs are—"

"Maybe I could go with you!" Miguel cried excitedly.

"No!" Leanna burst out. "I mean, it's just family."

"I understand," Miguel said, lacing his fingers through hers. "Besides, your father's so strict, he probably wouldn't approve of you bringing a guy home."

Leanna groaned. Why did Miguel remember *everything* she'd ever said? It made it harder to stick to the speech she'd rehearsed.

"Miguel," she began, "not everyone who looks Filipino observes all the customs and traditions."

"I know." He jerked the wheel, pulling the car around a corner. "Sometimes I get so angry at my younger brother and sister. Their haircuts, their clothes . . . I don't think they have any likes or dislikes of their own. They seem to do whatever their American friends tell them is cool."

"Well, it's fun doing things with your friends," Leanna said, forgetting her prepared speech. "I love modeling because Kelli and I do it together."

Miguel laughed shortly. "It doesn't surprise me that Kelli's into modeling."

"What's that supposed to mean?" Leanna demanded. She pulled her hand from Miguel's.

"All I meant was, Kelli's tall and pretty, so it figures she'd like modeling. You just don't seem the type, though."

"What type is that?" Leanna flung out. "Short and ugly?"

"You know you're not short and ugly." Miguel reached for the radio knob, blasting the car with country music. "How about some music?"

"Ugh! I hate this station."

Miguel switched off the radio. "What's the matter, Leanna? Why are you picking a fight?" he asked, sounding bewildered. "What did I do to upset you?"

"If you cared about me, you'd accept everything about me . . . even my modeling and my friends."

"I do accept them." Miguel's eyes were on the road. His jaw seemed to tighten. "I just don't understand them."

"Listen, there's a fashion show at the mall next Saturday." Leanna took a deep breath. "Kelli and I are in it, along with some of our friends from Bayside. I'd like you to come and watch."

"I might have to work." Miguel pulled into a crowded parking lot. "Here we are. Café Manila. Look for a good space."

With a sinking feeling, Leanna realized that Miguel hadn't said whether he'd go to the fashion show or not. *Well, we're even. I didn't tell him about my family, either.*

The fashion show will be a test, Leanna decided. *If Miguel shows up, I promise I'll tell him about the Van Havers afterward. And I won't wimp out, no matter what!*

As they walked through double doors into the restaurant where his parents worked, Leanna felt better, more relaxed. She'd decided to tell Miguel the truth, just not tonight.

"This place is packed," she said.

Miguel walked to the front of the line. "We won't have to wait for a table, though. My parents are expecting us."

Miguel gave his name to the Filipina hostess. She led them to a small table in the center of the room, near a U-shaped buffet.

"*Mabúhay!* Welcome to Café Manila," a red-headed waitress said. "We have a special Fiesta Buffet tonight. Or would you like to see a menu?"

"I'll have the buffet," Leanna decided.

"Me too," Miguel agreed. "It's the best way to sample lots of different foods—and we can come back for seconds and thirds."

"Great!" Leanna walked to the end of the buffet and picked up an empty plate. "*Gutom na ako.*"

"I'm hungry, too. Hey, you've been practicing Tagalog!" Miguel said proudly as he served a spoon full of steaming rice onto his plate.

As Miguel pulled into the Van Havers' driveway after their dinner, he lapsed into silence. He parked the car and turned toward Leanna. In the dim light from the twin globes on the Van Havers' garage, his face was all dark lines and shadows.

"Leanna," he began, "I need to say something."

Leanna froze, feeling all trembly inside. Miguel sounded so serious. What if he wanted to break up? What if he'd thought about the fashion show and already decided he wasn't interested? "I won't lie to you, Leanna."

She dropped her gaze. Could she ever say the same to him?

"Your modeling doesn't bother me. But Kelli Van Haver does." Miguel shook his head. "I don't like phony, superficial girls like her. And I can't understand why you do. But I'm willing to try." He brushed a strand of hair from her forehead and added, "Maybe we can all go out after the fashion show. You know, get to know one another."

Leanna's heart jumped. She leaned forward to kiss him, but the seat belt held her back. Miguel chuckled softly and reached across to unfasten it. Then they were in each other's arms.

"Mahal kita," Miguel whispered, just before his lips met hers.

I've got to remember to ask Carlos what that means, Leanna thought. Closing her eyes, she wished their good-night kiss could last forever.

Chapter Fifteen

THE NEXT SATURDAY afternoon, Miguel walked uncomfortably into the center court of the shopping mall.

The Arden Fair Mall was a steel-and-glass monster. Inside the mall, you couldn't tell what year it was, what country you were in, or even the season. Big silver snowflakes hung from the ceiling, and the banner across the center stage read Winter Fantasy Fashion Show, even though it was only a week before Halloween, and the temperature outside was almost eighty degrees.

The folding chairs near the stage were filling up fast with junior high and high school girls. Some were with their mothers or grandmothers. The only guys in the audience were a handful of fathers, grandfathers, and little brothers. Miguel felt as conspicuous as a giant wart on someone's face.

This wasn't his idea of fun. But being in the fashion show seemed really important to Leanna, so he wanted to support her and cheer her on.

And to be nice to Kelli Van Haver afterward. Don't forget that part. Miguel grimaced. He planned to give Kelli a chance, but would she give *him* one? The one time he'd spent more than five minutes with Kelli, she seemed to dislike him. Miguel was afraid Kelli would turn Leanna against him and everything Philippine, just like his sister's friends had done to her.

Miguel found a seat in the back, near the foot of a red-carpeted runway that extended out from the stage. He perched uncomfortably on the edge of his chair. To his left, two very young girls were talking loudly about their favorite lipsticks. Miguel rolled his eyes. He'd give anything to see a familiar face right now. Preferably a guy who'd talk about anything but makeup and clothes.

As if in answer to his wish, a tall, thin guy about Miguel's age stepped out from behind the glittering gold curtain. He was dressed all in black, except for his gray pin-striped vest and bright red tie. He carried a video camera and a tripod to the end of the runway and began setting them up.

The cameraman's blond hair and wire-rimmed glasses seemed familiar, but Miguel couldn't place where he knew him from.

After setting up the camera, the blond guy glanced into the audience. "Hey, man," he called down to Miguel, "can you keep an eye on my equipment for a minute?"

"Sure," Miguel happily agreed. *Whew, something to do.*

The tall blonde hurried up the runway and disappeared behind the curtain. A moment later he reappeared, carrying a long white cardboard box and a lamp on a pole.

"Thanks, man," he said to Miguel as he put down the box and began setting up the light. "I'm filming the show so the girls can watch it afterward and see what they did right and what they need to improve."

Miguel stood up and leaned his elbow on the runway, which was level with his chin. "Are you a professional photographer?" he asked. "You look kind of young to have a full-time job."

"This is just while I'm in high school." The cameraman finished adjusting his lamp and dropped to a sitting position on the red carpet. "I'm not sure if I want to be a director or a cameraman, but it'll be something behind the scenes. Are you interested in filmmaking, too?"

"I love *watching* movies," Miguel replied, "but I've never thought much about making them. I work at the Cinedome, so I get to see all the new movies as soon as they come out."

The guy snapped his fingers. "I thought you looked familiar! Weren't you there last night? I saw you mopping the floor."

"Yeah, that was me," Miguel admitted. "But I don't plan on mopping floors and selling popcorn all my life. I really want to study anthropology."

"Like, dig up old bones and stuff?"

"Maybe, but I'm also interested in modern-day people who still live as others did thousands of years ago. In the Philippines, where I was born, there are lots of tribes that still live that way. The Mangyans, the Ati, the Tasaday—"

"I've heard of the Tasaday. I'd give anything to be on the first crew to film an undiscovered tribe." His blue eyes glittered behind his glasses. "Maybe we could work together someday."

"Maybe." Miguel smiled and started back toward his seat.

"No, I really mean it." The blond guy leaned down and stuck out his hand. "I'm Scott. Scott Carteret."

"Miguel Sarmiento." Miguel shook hands with his new friend.

"Why don't you give me your number? We can hang out, and I'll show you some of my films . . . if you're interested. They're mostly documentaries," Scott said, sounding self-conscious. "Travel, history, interviews . . . you probably think that's weird."

"No. It sounds cool," Miguel replied.

Scott wrote Miguel'. phone number on a small notepad inside his wallet. "Maybe we can make a documentary on the Philippine experience in America," he said enthusiastically. "There's a girl in today's fasion show who'd be perfect for it. She's really photogenic. Here, see for yourself." Scott flipped open his wallet and held it out to Miguel.

Miguel glanced at the school picture—and felt

as if all the air had been knocked out of him with one swift, savage punch. He gripped the edge of the runway for support. What was *Leanna's* picture doing in another guy's wallet?

"That's—Leanna!" he gasped, pointing to Scott's wallet.

"You know her?" Scott asked. He sounded completely oblivious to Miguel's distress.

"I . . . I thought I did," Miguel said faintly. There had to be some mistake! "Is this the same Leanna who lives with the Van Havers?"

"*Lives* with the Van Havers?" Scott repeated. "She *is* a Van Haver! Leanna's only half Filipina. Mr. and Mrs. Van Haver are her mother and stepfather. Leanna's real dad lives in San Diego." Scott stuck his wallet back in his pocket and laughed. "You must not know Leanna that well."

"No . . . I hardly know her at all," Miguel said slowly. Scott, on the other hand, seemed to know Leanna *very* well. Scott had all this personal information about her family.

And he had her picture in his wallet!

"Where did you meet Leanna?" Scott's smile was still friendly, his voice still casual. He didn't sound jealous or suspicious at all.

"It doesn't matter," Miguel muttered. A whirlwind of emotions raced through his mind. He wanted to hate Scott, but he seemed like such a nice guy. Maybe Scott didn't know Leanna was two-timing him. He tried to hate Leanna, but his anger was overwhelmed by a burst of raw pain. The

153

only person Miguel really hated was himself. How could he have been stupid enough to trust Leanna, when she'd been lying to him from the minute they'd met?

"Is something wrong?" Scott asked, frowning. But just then he was interrupted by a burst of music. "Show's starting! Catch you later," Scott said, leaping to his feet. He turned on the camera as a tall, dark-haired woman in an evening gown emerged from behind the curtains and welcomed the audience to the Winter Fantasy Fashion Show.

Shaking his head in disgust, Miguel stumbled away from the stage and headed for the nearest exit. He no longer had any reason to stick around.

"How do I look?" Leanna asked nervously.

Kelli took in Leanna's bright red tights, black and white plaid kilt, and bulky red sweater with Scottie dogs romping around the neckline. "Like you're ready for your first day of kindergarten."

Leanna brushed a fleck of lint from her sweater. "At least I can sit down if I want to."

"Tell me about it," Kelli moaned. She was wearing a pure white angora sweater, and she was told not to sit or lean against anything while waiting her turn to go on.

"Do you think Miguel's out there?" Leanna asked. The girls had been stuck in the dressing room for the past hour and hadn't had a chance to peek out at the audience.

"He said he was coming, didn't he?" Kelli asked,

sounding annoyed. "From what you've told me, Miguel keeps his promises. Not like some of the losers I've dated."

"Girls! Time to line up!" A woman with a clipboard walked briskly through the dressing room, shooing the twelve models toward the door.

Kelli turned to follow, but Leanna grabbed her arm, risking damage to the white angora sweater.

"Places! Places!" the stage manager called, waving her clipboard frantically. Kelli and Leanna hurried into the wings with the others. Kelli took her place near the end of the line, and Leanna, who was the shortest, moved to the very front.

". . . proudly present our collection of casual wear, perfect for the schoolroom or the slopes."

That was Leanna's cue. Head high, she walked out of the wings with bouncy, energetic steps.

"Leanna is modeling a classic skirt and sweater ensemble from Cool Clothes," the emcee announced.

Leanna posed for a moment in front of the glittering gold curtain. Then, as the woman behind the microphone continued to talk about the outfit, Leanna started down the runway, pirouetting to show off her short flared skirt.

As she turned and smiled, her eyes swept the audience. She didn't see Miguel, but then, her eyes couldn't linger on any one section of seats. She had to keep moving and twirling. In seconds, her performance was over, and she rushed back to the dressing room to change into her next outfit—a hot pink ski suit.

155

Leanna was zipping up the jacket when Kelli ran into the dressing room a few minutes later. "I didn't see Miguel in the audience," Leanna said anxiously. "Did you?"

Kelli pulled the white sweater over her head. "No, but you were so into your act out there, you probably didn't notice Scott, either."

"Scott's here?" Leanna asked, tucking her hair into a pink knit cap. She hadn't been thinking about anyone but Miguel.

Kelli laughed. "See what I mean? He was right on the runway, filming, and you didn't even notice him."

The next time Leanna went out, she caught a glimpse of Scott's shadowy figure behind the camera. But she was too busy concentrating on her performance to pay much attention. While she was on the runway, she became a happy, energetic young girl on a ski trip. It was her job to convince everyone in the audience that if they bought this ski outfit, they could be happy and beautiful, too.

Only when the show was over, and Leanna was changing out of the hand-knitted sweater and dark green leggings she'd modeled last, did she have time to worry about Miguel again. "I still didn't see him, Kelli. What if he isn't here?"

"I'm sure he's out there." Kelli grabbed a handful of tissues and wiped the heavy stage makeup from her face. "And if he didn't make it, I'm sure he has a good reason. That awful car of his probably broke down."

"I hope not." Leanna pulled her own teal sweat-shirt over her head.

"Or he could have been in an accident," Kelli went on, tossing the tissues into a wastebasket.

Leanna shuddered. "You think of the worst things! Maybe he just decided to dump me."

"Not likely." Kelli ran a brush through Leanna's hair, then began to French braid it. "Guys dump *me*. They don't dump you. You always get the sweet, loyal boyfriends."

Leanna twisted her head around to stare at Kelli in amazement. "How do you know? Miguel is only the second guy I've ever dated."

"Turn around! You're messing up your hair," Kelli ordered. Leanna obeyed, and Kelli's fingers moved swiftly, arranging the silky dark hair in a neat braid. "You didn't go out with any guy who came along," Kelli explained. "I was so afraid of being alone that I said yes to everyone who asked. But you waited for the good ones. Guys like Scott, who I could never have in a million years."

"You like *Scott*?" Leanna asked. "Then why didn't you go out with him?"

"He never asked." Kelli sounded irritated, as if an idiot should have known the answer. "I wouldn't be surprised if Scott regrets breaking up with you. He's probably waiting for his chance to kiss and make up."

"I don't think so. Scott and I were more like buddies who liked to hang out. There were no sparks between us," Leanna admitted. She grabbed her purse from the back of a folding chair. "Anyway . . . Miguel's probably starving by now. I know I am. Let's go!"

Leanna hurried out into the mall, hoping Miguel was waiting for her. But all the folding chairs around the stage were empty. That is . . . all but one.

Scott jumped to his feet and headed toward Leanna, a big smile on his face . . . and a bouquet of pink carnations in his arms.

Chapter Sixteen

"GO ON, BREAK Scott's heart again—if you dare. I'll wait for you in the car." Kelli gave Leanna a push, then hurried off.

Leanna squared her shoulders and walked slowly toward Scott. She planned to make it perfectly clear that she was his friend, and nothing more.

"Where's Kelli going?" Scott asked, watching her head for the exit.

"She's meeting me outside." Leanna sat down on an empty folding chair. "I need to talk to you alone."

Scott sank into a nearby chair, placing the bouquet on the empty seat between them. "Okay. What's up?"

Leanna took a deep breath. "Scott, we've been through this before. I just don't think we work together as boyfriend and girlfriend. And I can't accept these flowers." Leanna touched the pink bouquet on the seat between them.

"That's good, because they're not for you." Scott's face had turned as pink as the flowers. "Kelli's not allergic to carnations, is she?"

"Not that I know of," Leanna answered absently. Then the meaning of his words sank in, and her eyes widened. "You like Kelli?"

Scott's face got redder. Even the tips of his ears were hot pink. "Well . . . yeah," he said. "I've liked Kelli for a long time. But she always goes out with big shots like Glenn Garrick, so I figured she'd never go out with me."

"So the whole time we dated, you were just *using* me?" Leanna punched Scott's arm playfully. "I can't believe you!"

Scott fiddled with the buttons on his antique vest. "I wouldn't put it that way," he mumbled. "Until I went out with you, I thought I was a loser when it came to girls. I never even considered asking Kelli out. It would have been like—like asking out a movie star or something. Then you came along. A pretty, popular girl who was nice to me. I'll always be grateful to you for giving me confidence in myself."

Scott didn't look confident, though. He looked pretty miserable, Leanna thought.

"Kelli and I—oh, it's probably hopeless," he muttered, pushing his glasses up. "But I've got to try."

Leanna put her hand on his shoulder. "It's not as hopeless as you think."

"What do you mean?" Scott's head snapped up,

160

his eyes gleaming wildly with hope. "Does Kelli like me?"

Leanna laughed. "I think you should ask her yourself."

Scott's thin face glowed with joy. "Thanks, Leanna! Thanks for everything!"

Suddenly he lunged across the empty seat, half-crushing the flowers, and gathered Leanna into his arms. It was an awkward, brotherly hug, and Leanna couldn't help laughing. She patted Scott on the shoulder . . . and then the laughter died in her throat as she saw Miguel sitting several rows behind them, his arms folded across his chest. He was glaring at her and Scott with hatred in his eyes.

"Scott!" Leanna gasped, struggling out of his embrace. "Miguel—"

"Oh, hey, this guy named Miguel was here earlier. He seemed to think you were an exchange student or something, but I set him straight." Scott caught sight of Miguel heading toward the exit. "Hey, there he is. Miguel!" Scott raised his voice and waved. "Hey, buddy, over here!"

Miguel turned to face them, then shot them a look of pure scorn. Leanna felt as if a poisoned dart had pierced her chest. Without a word, Miguel turned again and stalked toward the mall exit.

"What's his problem?" Scott asked.

"Miguel, wait!" Leanna yelled. She jumped up and ran after him. "Don't leave! I can explain!"

She caught up to Miguel just before he stormed out the door.

161

Folding his arms, Miguel leaned against the wall. "This should be good for a laugh," he said. His lip curled unpleasantly. "What part do you want to explain first, Leanna? The fact that you're a Van Haver, or the fact that you're going out with Scott?"

"I'm not dating Scott." Leanna planted herself in front of Miguel. "We broke up weeks ago. We're just friends."

"Right," Miguel sneered. "Do you hug all your friends like that?"

"Go ask Scott. He'll tell you the same thing."

Miguel's lips twisted into a bitter smile. "That's not good enough. You've gotten your friends—and relatives—to lie for you before."

"You're right," Leanna admitted. It was time to be honest. "I've told you a lot of lies, Miguel, but I'm asking you to forgive me. I love you—and that's the truth."

For a moment, the hard lines of his face almost seemed to soften. But then he snapped, "Love! What do you know about love?"

Leanna's eyes blurred with tears. She blinked them back and plunged recklessly on. "I know that you love me. I found out what *mahal kita* means. And you wouldn't say I love you if you didn't mean it. Please give me another chance."

"You've got to be kidding. How can you ask me to trust you?" Miguel shouted, his eyes flashing angrily. "You lied to me. You turned your back on your own family to get what you wanted. You're so self-absorbed, you don't even realize what you've done."

He started to walk away, but Leanna clutched his arm. "I can explain," she began.

"Don't touch me," Miguel snapped. His voice was so icy that Leanna quickly stepped back. Staring through Leanna as if she weren't there, Miguel pushed the exit door and stormed out of the mall.

Leanna took a deep, shaky breath, willing herself not to cry. It was strange, but suddenly there was only a huge, empty place in her chest, as if half her heart had been torn away. The rest of her felt numb and cold.

"Hey, Leanna, are you okay?" Scott walked up, an anxious expression on his face. "What was that all about?"

"Just a little misunderstanding," Leanna said, lifting her chin defiantly. "Miguel and I were going out for pizza, but it seems he's changed his mind. That's good news for you, Scott. Kelli was going to come with us, and now she's totally free. Wait here—I'll go get her!"

Leanna ran outside, half-hoping she'd see Miguel and his clunky station wagon. But the parking lot was enormous, and so many people rushed back and forth on the sidewalk that Miguel had already vanished into the crowd.

Miguel will be back, Leanna thought. He'd call after he'd had a chance to cool off. Or would he?

Leanna spent the rest of the afternoon at home, studying her English-Tagalog dictionary. Listening to the tapes was easier, but Leanna didn't want to wear headphones, afraid she'd miss Miguel's call.

But the phone never rang. Finally, Leanna slammed the book shut. *I'll call him,* she decided. The worst he could do was hang up.

Leanna clutched the receiver. The phone rang three, four, five times. *He's not home,* she thought, half-disappointed, half-relieved. But just as she was about to hang up, she heard a boy's voice on the line.

"Hello? Who's there?"

He doesn't sound angry, Leanna thought. She felt a surge of hope. Before she lost her nerve, Leanna took a deep breath and quickly began speaking. "Miguel, hi. It's Leanna. I'm really sorry. I didn't mean to——"

"Hold on," the voice interrupted. "This is Ramon. My brother Miguel's at work. Want me to take a message?"

"Uh, no thanks." Leanna replaced the receiver as a sob welled up in her throat. Ramon sounded so much like Miguel!

She couldn't wait till Miguel got off work. She had to do something now. She marched into the den and found her stepfather playing a computer game.

"Hi, Dad. Can I borrow your car? I want to go to the mall and pick up some new lipstick." Leanna asked sweetly.

"Sure, honey. Drive carefully," Dad said absently. His eyes were on the screen, where an animated muscle man was swimming across a river as flying lizards swooped down to attack him.

Leanna was halfway out the door when Dad called, "Wait! What about dinner? Kelli and your mom should be home in an hour. I thought it might be fun to try a recipe from that Philippine cookbook I brought home yesterday."

"I won't be long," Leanna promised. She'd catch Miguel at work and he'd have to listen. He wouldn't be able to hang up or walk away.

Miguel had been at work less than an hour, but already he wished he'd called in sick. He couldn't get Leanna out of his mind. It was hard to believe how quickly things had changed. One minute, he'd thought Leanna was the best thing that had ever happened to him. The next, he'd seen her picture in some other guy's wallet and found out she'd lied to him from the minute they'd met.

Two-timing was bad enough, but pretending to be someone she wasn't was unforgivable. By lying about her Philippine background, Leanna was mocking everything important to Miguel. He was glad he didn't have to face her again.

"Hey!" a teenage boy at the counter shouted. "I ordered a cherry cola. This is diet regular."

"Sorry," Miguel apologized, hastily replacing the soda. The boy grabbed it and hurried through the doors of Cinema Three. Miguel poured the rejected drink down the drain. When he turned away from the sink, he heard his two coworkers snickering.

"Seems like you can't keep your mind on your

work today," Tom said as he reached into the pop-corn machine and stuffed a handful into his mouth.

"Better be careful," Danette warned Miguel. "Messing up orders could get you fired."

"You'd like that, wouldn't you?" Miguel whirled furiously on the redheaded girl. "You're always on my case! Just chill out for once."

Danette shrank back against Tom. Her eyes widened in fake fear. "Tom, save me! He's flipping out!"

Miguel turned away, shaking his head in disgust. Knowing Danette, she'd probably go to the manager with some exaggerated story about how he'd "attacked" her. Just what he needed. The perfect ending to a rotten day.

And it wasn't over yet. A bunch of customers descended on the snack bar, and for a few minutes Miguel was too busy filling orders to think about Leanna and her lies. Then he burned his thumb on a bowl of hot nachos. As he rushed to the sink and plunged his thumb into the stream of cold water, Miguel couldn't believe how badly it hurt. The skin was already starting to blister.

"What else can go wrong?" he groaned, just as he heard Danette's shrill voice.

"Miguel! Customer at the register!"

He was tempted to tell Danette to take care of it herself. But Miguel glanced around and saw that, for once, Tom and Danette were as busy as he was. Tom was pouring drinks, and Danette was filling several bags with popcorn.

Sighing, Miguel dried his throbbing thumb and

approached the cash register. "May I help—oh, man. What are you doing here?"

Leanna Malig—no, Leanna *Van Haver*—was standing at the counter near the register. She was twisting the end of her French braid and biting her lip, and not quite meeting his eyes.

"What do you want?" he snapped.

"I—I want to talk to you," Leanna stammered. She shrank back a little.

"We have nothing to talk about," Miguel said coldly. "Do you want some popcorn or something?"

"No. It's bad enough I had to buy a ticket into the theater just to see you," Leanna said. "I can't stop thinking about you. Can't you give me another chance?"

Suddenly Danette appeared beside him. "Miguel," she said sternly, "I've told you to leave your personal life at home. Work is no place to talk to your girlfriend."

"She's not my girlfriend!" Miguel snarled.

"Miguel, we really need to talk," Leanna continued.

Couldn't she see she was getting him into trouble? Probably not, Miguel thought. As usual, Leanna was only thinking about herself.

"I told you before, I have nothing to say to you," Miguel said roughly.

"But—"

"No!" Miguel burst out. "Do you understand the word *'no'?* Or is that another word—like love or truth—that you just don't get?"

Leanna's face flushed. "Fine!" she cried. "If that's how you feel, I'm out of here. You're not the only guy in the world."

As Leanna stalked out without a backward glance, Miguel realized that he'd gone too far. He knew he wouldn't be seeing Leanna again.

Good, Miguel thought. *That's exactly the way I want it.*

Chapter Seventeen

"**N**o," MIGUEL SAID into the telephone. "No way. Absolutely not."

It was Saturday morning, two weeks since he'd uncovered Leanna's lies. Miguel had never expected to see Leanna or anyone connected with her again. He could hardly believe that Scott, of all people, had called him on the phone. Even more incredibly, that Scott had had the nerve to ask him for a favor.

"Look, I wouldn't ask if there were any other way," Scott said. "But my car won't start. My parents are away, and everyone else I know either isn't home or is at the fashion show already. They're counting on me, man. If I don't show up, there'll be nobody to film the show."

"Can't you take a cab?" Miguel asked. He knew he sounded cold, but what did Scott expect? The guy had more guts than brains, asking him for a ride!

"My equipment won't fit in a cab, and I could really use your help carrying it around. Besides, I'm broke," Scott said. "If you give me a hand, I'll split the money I get from this job. I know we've never hung out or anything, but I thought you were cool. C'mon, man, do me this favor and I'll owe you big."

"I don't know," Miguel said. He found himself wanting to help Scott, and he could use some extra cash to buy new seat covers for his car. But fashion shows weren't on his list of top ten activities, and he definitely didn't want to run into Leanna.

As if reading his mind, Scott said, "If this is about Leanna, you don't have to avoid me because of her. Leanna and I broke up a long time ago. In fact, I'm dating Kelli."

Miguel's eyebrows rose. He didn't understand Scott's taste in girls. *Both* Van Haver girls were bad news.

"Thanks for telling me," Miguel said. He felt a little better, knowing Scott and Leanna weren't dating, but that still didn't erase her other lies. "But I'm not interested in Leanna anymore. Seeing her at the fashion show could be kind of . . . awkward, know what I mean?"

"Don't worry about that. This is a men's fashion show. All guys," Scott explained. "Leanna's not in it and won't even be there. Kelli has a major photo shoot in San Francisco today, and Leanna went along to help with her makeup."

For a moment, Miguel wondered if this were

some kind of setup. Maybe Leanna had asked Scott to call, to trick Miguel into attending this supposedly all–male fashion show, where Leanna would be waiting. Devious plans were Leanna's style.

Knock it off, Miguel told himself. Guys didn't do favors like that for their ex-girlfriends. He was really losing it if he believed Leanna was behind all this. Scott sounded desperate for a ride, and Leanna didn't care enough to try any complicated stunts to win Miguel back.

"Okay, I'll do it." Miguel sighed. As Scott gave him directions to his house, Miguel wondered if he was making a major mistake.

"Hey, Leanna." Glenn Garrick's voice on the phone was superconfident, as always. "If you're not busy today, how about coming to the fashion show at Memorial Auditorium? In exchange for helping me with my hair, I'll take you to the best restaurant in town afterward."

Leanna rolled her eyes. Glenn thought every girl in the world was dying to go out with him. But no matter how many times she said "No," Glenn never got the hint.

"Gee, Glenn, that sounds wonderful," Leanna replied in a deadpan voice. "But why do I get the honor of styling your hair? Is your mother out of town?"

"Actually, she's in L.A., showing my portfolio to an agent." Glenn's voice rose excitedly, as it always did when he talked about himself. "Mom thinks

I'm wasting my potential at Bayside. She thinks I've got a shot at Hollywood. By next year, you'll be seeing me on the big screen!"

As Glenn went on about his chance at stardom, Leanna covered the mouthpiece. "Glenn Garrick," she told Kelli, DeShaun, and Sara, who were packing some snacks for the drive to San Francisco. "He's either asking me out, or hiring me as his hairdresser, I'm not sure which."

"Go for it!" Sara said. "Glenn's so cute, so sexy—"

"So dumb, so conceited," DeShaun went on. "I thought you were coming to San Francisco with us."

"So, can I pick you up in an hour?" Glenn asked.

"Hold on just a second," Leanna told him.

"Well, okay." Glenn sounded irritated, as if he couldn't understand why anyone would have to think twice about accepting an invitation from him.

Leanna put her hand over the mouthpiece again. An image of herself shouting at Miguel "You're not the only guy in the world!" flashed through her mind. She'd been so angry, she'd sworn to go out with the first guy who'd asked her. But was she desperate enough to go out with *Glenn*?

"What do you think?" she asked Kelli.

"Glenn's fun, as long as you don't fall for him," Kelli said. She put another apple inside her knapsack. "Maybe if you go out with Glenn, you'll stop moping about Miguel."

"That's for sure," DeShaun snorted. She slammed the refrigerator. "Trust me, Glenn won't let you think about anyone but Glenn, Glenn, Glenn. By the time you get home, you won't remember your *own* name, let alone Miguel's."

Leanna laughed bitterly. "That's exactly what I need." She uncovered the mouthpiece and said, "Okay, Glenn. Pick me up in an hour."

"Miguel, could you plug in that lamp?" Scott asked. Miguel was helping him set up the movie camera and lighting equipment on the stage at Memorial Auditorium in downtown Sacramento.

Miguel picked up the plug and headed for the nearest socket. "The cord won't reach," he told Scott. "Can I move the lamp about six inches to the left?"

"No good," Scott replied. He began unfolding a tripod. "That lamp has to be exactly where it is or we'll get too much glare on the models' faces. Did we bring an extension cord?"

Miguel glanced quickly at the jumble of equipment. "I don't see one."

"How could I have been so stupid?" Scott groaned, raking his fingers through his blond hair. "Okay, see if you can find the custodian backstage. Maybe he's got an extension cord."

Miguel pushed aside the heavy velvet draperies and ducked between them. The backstage area was chaos. There were tons of guys wandering around . . . and they were wearing *makeup*. Miguel would never understand this modeling thing.

He stopped a tall man carrying a clipboard.

"Excuse me, do you know where the custodian is?"

The man peered at Miguel through round tinted glasses. "No, but who are you? Are you one of the models?"

"I'm helping Scott Carteret," Miguel said quickly. "I'm looking for an extension cord."

"Check the supply closet down that hall." The guy pointed with his clipboard. "But wait! Have you ever done any modeling? TV commercials?"

"No," Miguel said. He started backing away.

The guy with the clipboard followed. "You have a great look! Have you ever thought about modeling?"

Miguel shook his head. "Actually, all I'd like to do is find an extension cord."

"Okay, but if you change your mind, give me a call."

The man pressed a business card into Miguel's hand. Miguel glanced down at the block letters. TYRONE ASHBY, TALENT AGENT.

Miguel shook his head. This was too weird. Mr. Ashby began herding the models into a line, and Miguel looked for a wastebasket. He didn't see one, so he tucked the card into his pocket and headed down the hallway.

He passed a couple of dressing rooms filled with guys adjusting their ties or running combs through their hair. The next three doors were closed. The first was clearly marked as a bathroom, but one of the others could have been the supply closet.

Miguel knocked on one of the doors. When no one answered, he turned the knob and pushed the door open.

He immediately realized his mistake. He'd blundered into another dressing room. The guy inside, standing on the opposite side of the room with his back to the door, apparently hadn't heard Miguel knock because he was talking in a loud voice. "So, I'm heading to Hollywood as soon as Mom decides which agent to sign with. They all want me, you know, so it's just a question of who'll offer the best deal. I'll finish high school with a private tutor, and afterward . . . well, who needs college when you're a star?"

Miguel knew he should leave the room immediately, but he couldn't help staring at the guy. He seemed to be talking to himself. He hadn't paused for a breath and no one in the room was talking back. Yet there *was* someone else there. A girl. Most of her was hidden behind the speaker's broad-shouldered body. Every so often, Miguel saw a flash of slender hands reaching up, fussing with the front of the guy's light brown hair.

"Glenn, hold still!" The girl's voice suddenly cut through the speaker's monologue. "If you don't stop wriggling, I might burn you with this curling iron!"

Miguel's blood turned to boiling acid. Leanna! She hadn't wasted any time getting a new boyfriend. Miguel had to see what this loser looked like.

"Excuse me," Miguel said, walking toward the couple. "Can you help me find the supply closet?"

Glenn turned around. He really *did* look like an actor.

"This isn't the supply closet," Glenn said arrogantly. "Get lost."

"But I'm already lost," Miguel said cheerfully. He was ignoring Glenn now and watching Leanna for some sort of reaction. Her face was totally drained of color, and her almond eyes were so wide, they almost seemed round.

She looked astonished, a little uneasy, Miguel thought with satisfaction.

And absolutely beautiful.

"What are you doing here?" Leanna gasped.

"Looking for an extension cord," Miguel replied. He pointed to the white cord connecting the curling iron to the outlet. "How about that one?"

"No! That's mine," Glenn said indignantly. "Leanna, you only put one wave in my hair. I asked for two."

"Hey, Leanna, you never did my hair when we were dating," Miguel said. He leaned against the wall, almost in Leanna's face, and ruffled his bangs with his fingers. "What do you think? Do I need conditioner?"

Miguel wasn't sure what he was trying to prove. He only knew that he had a sudden, irresistible urge to be as annoying as possible. He couldn't stand seeing Leanna so close to Glenn, touching his hair. If he could goad Leanna into losing her temper, Miguel hoped he'd be able to hate her again, instead of wanting her back.

His plan seemed to be working.

"Get out of here," Leanna said coldly. She

started to make a second wave in Glenn's hair.

"You used to go out with this janitor?" Glenn asked Leanna. He acted as if Miguel wasn't even there.

"I'm not a janitor," Miguel said. "I'm helping Scott with the lights."

"Yeah?" Glenn's hair was finished, and he turned to Miguel. "Make sure you keep that spotlight on me, boy. I'm the star of this show."

"You may be the star," Miguel said, his voice low, "but I'm not your 'boy.'"

"I can say whatever I want," Glenn shot back. "My parents pay taxes, but you immigrants sneak into this country illegally and take jobs away from Americans. Do you want me to call Immigration?"

Miguel couldn't believe how ignorant Glenn was. He was trying to decide if he should argue with Glenn, laugh at him, or just walk away, when Leanna, who'd been standing there silently, suddenly stepped between them.

"I can't believe you, Glenn." Leanna's back was to Miguel, but from the set of her shoulders and her tone of voice, Miguel could imagine the angry look on her face. "Miguel's not an 'immigrant.' His family came here from the Philippines, and—"

Glenn's nostrils flared. "These foreigners are taking over the country. It makes me sick!"

"I'm a Filipina and I'm proud of it!" Leanna, hands on her hips, was shouting in Glenn's face. "Do I make you sick, Glenn?"

"Of course not!" Glenn looked genuinely

shocked. "You were born here. I'm talking about people who come from other countries. Most of them go on welfare and they run down the neighborhoods and commit crimes. Why should they have the same rights as American citizens?"

"Because we're human beings," Leanna said.

Miguel noticed that Leanna had put herself in the same category—and there was no mistaking her sincerity. She wasn't trying to impress him. She was speaking from the heart.

"It's not where you come from that matters," Leanna told Glenn. "It's what kind of person you are inside. Miguel's honest and hardworking, but you're a conceited jerk!"

"What's going on in here?" a new voice demanded. The agent, Tyrone Ashby, appeared in the doorway. "Five minutes to curtain time! Glenn, get out there!"

"I'm outta here, all right," Glenn said. He plucked a duffel bag from the floor and began stuffing hairbrushes and makeup inside. "You can have your crummy show without me!"

Tyrone rushed over to Glenn, begging him not to let his personal problems interfere with his job.

Miguel barely noticed Glenn or the agent. All his attention was on Leanna. She turned to him, tears glistening in her eyes.

"Miguel, I'm sorry I lied to you," she said. "I know you'll never forgive me. But I wanted to say thank you. Because of you, I've learned to love my Philippine

178

heritage. I hope someday we can be friends."

A lump rose in Miguel's throat, and he knew, suddenly, that friendship would never be enough. "Leanna," he began. But then he felt his body slam into the wall as Glenn pushed roughly past on his way out the door. Miguel had barely caught his breath when Tyrone grabbed his arm.

"You've got to take Glenn's place!" Tyrone cried. "You've got the right build, the same shoulders—we can hem the pants with adhesive tape—"

"Miguel hates modeling," Leanna said. "He won't do it . . . will you, Miguel?"

Suddenly Miguel knew he'd do whatever it took to make Leanna smile. Besides, it was partly his fault that Glenn had walked out of the fashion show in the first place. If Miguel refused to fill in, lots of people would be disappointed.

"Okay," he said. "But no makeup."

"No time for makeup." Tyrone dragged Miguel toward a rack of clothes. "Leanna, go tell them to delay the curtain."

"Leanna!" Miguel called. "Wait a second!"

"What?" she asked, looking hopeful.

"You can talk to her later!" Tyrone almost shrieked. "Put on this suit!"

Miguel pointed to the curling iron that Glenn had left behind. "The extension cord—give it to Scott!"

"Okay," Leanna said in a small voice. From her disappointed expression, Miguel could tell she'd been hoping he'd say something else.

★   ★   ★

179

Miguel looks great up there, Leanna thought. He moved gracefully, and his broad shoulders and narrow hips were perfect for showing off the designer suits he modeled. Of course, his white tennis shoes looked bizarre with the three-piece suits, but Leanna hoped no one else in the audience noticed.

The first time Miguel walked down the runway, he seemed nervous. But each time he came out, he seemed to loosen up, until his pained grimace became a genuine smile.

Am I seeing things? Leanna wondered. Miguel looked as if he were enjoying himself! The last time he came out, Miguel was actually strutting! Best of all, as he moved in time with the music, his eyes never left Leanna's. He seemed to be doing this just for her.

When the show ended, Leanna hurried backstage. She found Miguel standing in the doorway of his dressing room, talking to Tyrone. Leanna's knees felt weak.

But then Miguel looked directly at her. *Rescue me,* his eyes seemed to say.

Leanna walked over to him.

"There you are!" Miguel said. "Excuse us, Tyrone. We're late for—uh—something."

"What was that all about?" Leanna asked as she followed Miguel down the hallway.

"Tyrone keeps saying I have 'The Look,' whatever that is. He wants me to enroll at Bayside and major in modeling. But that's not important right now." Miguel yanked open the first door he came to and stepped inside. "Come here, I need to talk to you."

"In a broom closet?" Leanna asked, stepping into a small room filled with mops, brooms, and shelves of cleaning supplies.

"I guess it's not the most romantic spot," Miguel said. "But, then, this isn't the worst mistake I've made. My worst mistake was breaking up with you."

Leanna caught her breath. She leaned back against the shelves. "You—you forgive me?"

"I was wrong, too, Leanna." Miguel swallowed hard. "When you said those things to Glenn, I realized I was just as prejudiced as he was. I wanted you to be part of *my* world, but I wasn't ready to accept yours. I didn't respect the things that were important to you."

"I didn't give you the chance to know what was important to me, except, of course, my modeling."

Miguel's face turned crimson. "I felt pretty good out on that runway," he admitted. "I see why you like it. Not that I'm ready to enroll at Bayside—"

"But you have 'The Look,'" Leanna teased. She took a step closer. She couldn't keep her hand from trembling as she reached out and brushed Miguel's silky bangs back from his forehead. "All you need are some curls here . . . and here."

Leanna felt Miguel's arms tighten around her waist. She trailed a finger down his smooth cheek, lingering on his strong chin.

"Leanna," Miguel began, "can we give it another

try? I'm ready to make some compromises. Like, we can go out for burgers and fries one night as long as the next night we can have oxtail stew—"

"I'm willing if you are," Leanna said. "I'm a Filipina, but I'm an American, too. I'd like us to explore both cultures. Together." Leanna took a deep breath and hoped she'd get her pronunciation right. "*Mahal kita*, Miguel."

Surprise and pleasure lit Miguel's dark eyes. "I love you, too," he said. And he sealed it with a kiss.

Do you ever wonder about falling in love? About members of the opposite sex? Do you need a little friendly advice but have no one to turn to? Well, that's where we come in . . . Jenny and Jake. Send us those questions you're dying to ask, and we'll give you the straight scoop on life and love in the nineties.

DEAR JAKE

Q: *My boyfriend and I have been dating for more than a year now, and we really love each other. But lately we've been fighting all the time. You see, my boyfriend hates the way I dress. He buys me clothes a lot—really sexy clothes—and I like to wear them. But sometimes I just want to relax and wear jeans and my favorite sweatshirt. Last weekend my boyfriend came over to watch a video and he insisted that I change. He said I looked like a grandmother! I know he loves me, but recently all he does is hurt my feelings. What should I do?*

AS, Chicago, IL

A: Who does your boyfriend think he is—Calvin Klein? Tell him that it really hurts when he criticizes your appearance. Then stand up for yourself. Don't allow him to dictate your wardrobe. Teach your boyfriend about the art of compromise. You'll wear those silver vinyl pants when you go out, but he's got to understand your need for comfortable clothes, too. Your boyfriend can't pick and choose which parts of you he wants to love. If he can't accept you for who you are, then maybe you should go out and find someone who will.

Q: *There's this guy—I'll call him Ryan. We've been friends for the past few years. Then suddenly we became more* than just friends. We started talking a lot at school and on the phone. Ryan always says how cool he thinks I am. And he finally admitted that he likes me. I'm stunned and I realize that I care about him, too. But Ryan's so shy that he hung up the phone a second after he told me how he feels. He didn't even wait to hear my response. And the worst part is that he's been ignoring me ever since. Whenever I walk past him and his friends at school, I can hear them laughing. Was this all just a big joke to him, or does he really like me?

EB, Ardmore, OK

A: Instead of walking past Ryan and wondering what he's thinking, why don't you ask him? He put himself out on a limb when he shared his feelings, so now it's your turn. Is it possible that he thinks *you're* ignoring *him*? He's probably feeling very vulnerable and is just waiting for a sign from you. If you're not comfortable confronting him at school, call him up or write him a letter. Statistically speaking, it's extremely unlikely that Ryan expressed romantic interest in you as a practical joke. But it's time you get to the bottom of this and find out for sure.

DEAR JENNY

Q: *Last week Tim asked me out. Normally I'd be psyched to have a date, but there's one major problem here. All of my friends are pressuring me to say no because Tim is fat. Even my best friend is making fun of me. She says this guy is a loser and she can't believe that I'm even thinking about going out with him. She's making me feel really bad and now I'm totally embarrassed about the whole thing. I don't think it should matter if*

Tim's fat or not, but I need another girl's opinion. What do you think, Jenny?

SA, Blue Springs, MO

A: You're absolutely right—what your friends think is not important and neither is Tim's body fat percentage. Attraction is a very personal thing. One girl's "huge and hairy" is another girl's "cute and cuddly." What matters is how *you* feel about him. As for your best friend—she needs a major attitude adjustment. A friend should never make you feel bad or embarrassed. It sounds like she's jealous. Maybe she feels left out because this boy is calling you, not her. Also, she might resent that he's taking your attention away from her. Tell your friend to butt out of your business. This is a case where that old saying is true. . . . If she doesn't have anything nice to say, she shouldn't say anything at all.

Q: *Rob and I have been going out for almost two years, and we got engaged last August. Everything was great until Rob decided to go into the army. He's leaving in one month! I know he's going because he needs the money, and he's really psyched to be in Special Forces. What can I do to make the time go faster while he's gone? If anything happens to him, my life will be over.*

SH, Loganville, GA

A: It's very hard to have to part—even temporarily— from someone you love. You can still keep in touch with your fiancé by calling him, writing letters, and sending care packages. But you should also use this time apart to take care of yourself. Even though you love him very much, your fiancé shouldn't be your whole world. Use this opportunity to pursue your own interests. Take a class or read a book that you've always been curious about but never had time for in the past. Join a club. Get involved with your local community center. Above all, keep busy. Then, when your fiancé comes home to visit, surprise him with all you've learned and accomplished while he was gone!

Do you have questions about love? Write to:

Jenny Burgess or Jake Korman
c/o Daniel Weiss Associates
33 West 17th Street
New York, NY 10011